Coming Home

IAN FORTUNE-WOOD

CinnamonPress
INDEPENDENT INNOVATIVE INTERNATIONAL

Published by Cinnamon Press
Meirion House
Glan yr afon
Tanygrisiau
Blaenau Ffestiniog
Gwynedd LL41 3SU
www.cinnamonpress.com

The right of Jan Fortune-Wood to be identified as author
of this work has been asserted by her in accordance with
the Copyright, Designs and Patent Act, 1988. © 2011 Jan
Fortune-Wood. ISBN 978-1-907090-27-1
British Library Cataloguing in Publication Data. A CIP
record for this book can be obtained from the British
Library

Designed and typeset in Palatino and Garamond by
Cinnamon Press. Cover design by Jan Fortune-Wood from
original artwork, 'Cottage' © Stendec, agency:
dreamstime.com

Printed in Poland

The publisher acknowledges the financial assistance of the
Welsh Books Council.

Acknowledgements

With thanks to all those who helped along the way, especially to Anthony Delgrado, John Griffiths and Ann Drysdale, for their support and feedback; to my family for continually supporting my writing and to Sue Cvach, for more than I can say.

for Maria, James & Rose

Coming Home

July

Megan stands by the half-drawn living room curtains. Outside the sky is clear, a cloudless pale blue with the promise of heat. She grips the thick red cotton fabric, and shouts, 'Ben!'

'God, Megan, what's wrong? Ben crosses the small living room. He stretches his broad palm across her shoulder blades, and begins to knead; a familiar reflex of reassurance.

'It's… Look Ben… In that car…' Megan waves her small hand limply.

'Bloody hell!'

Megan watches her father doze in the red car parked outside her neat new Docklands house. His hair is still black, she sees, but why would it change dramatically in eighteen months? Has it really been only eighteen months? His skin looks more leathery, darker than ever after Africa, Manila, places she cannot imagine. In his sleep, head flung back, square jaw slightly open, Megan thinks he looks like an off-duty Roman centurion. She feels her world tilt; jolt her back:

'Your Nain died,' Mam says flatly as eight-year-old Megan flops onto the sofa after school.

Nain died. At the words her dad, who is pacing the room, yelps like a dog whose paw has been trodden on. He stands still, clutches his stomach and weeps; her silent dad howls. She has never seen Tada sob before. He stands and sits, sits and stands, helpless and confused, while her mam folds her head into her hands and rocks silently back and forth. Outside, the sky is like wet ash; moist grey clumps that will soon rain down on them, drenching the world with the dissolved grime of slate and coal.

Megan knows there will be a service, and that she will not be allowed to go. It will be her dad's brothers and sisters, Taid and all the great uncles and great aunts with their yellowing eyes and old people's breath. They will be the ones at the chapel, singing the psalm that her Nain taught her about the shadow of death. Afterwards they will all drink together in the King's Head in Blaenau, where the Royal Welch Fusiliers meet. There are no children allowed, except at Christmas, when they are lined up at long tables and instructed to enjoy themselves, gorging on cheap cake and slimy jelly eaten through the din of party whistles.

'Don't say anything to Elin,' her mam adds. Megan knows without asking that Elin is too little to be told anything; Elin doesn't know what it means to be dead.

Megan tiptoes to her room and sits on the scratchy nylon
bedspread with its fat pink and orange flowers. She searches through the Bible Nain gave her and finds the right psalm. Its floppy black cover is cool against her sticky palms. The gold edges of the hair-thin pages still smell of Nain's tickly smoke.

At night her tada comes into her bedroom and takes the Bible out of her hands. He lifts the black leather to his face for a moment.

'It's a bit miserable to be reading this right now, Cariad.' He jerks his jaw towards the Bible and puts the book down by the lamp, its clear plastic base filled with pink flowers. 'You should read something a bit more cheerful.' Tada's hand lingers on her red hair.

His eyes are reddened and Megan can smell work on his hands, rough from car engines and slate mines. Tada turns out the lamp and goes out onto the landing.

Her tada, who works long shifts at the Oakley mine and sleeps whenever he gets the chance, stops sleeping. Instead he paces the landing at night and sobs, the tears silent until they make him choke. Outside, the rain beats against the house, sulphured from all the coal that burns in every chimney.

On a night just after Christmas, when everyone cries remembering how Nain cooked the turkey just right, Nain laid the table, Nain wrapped the gifts, Megan has a nosebleed. She passes her tada, who is staring out of the landing window at the top of the stairs. Megan thinks he looks as strong as the Roman centurions she is learning about at school, the ones who first mined slate near Caernarfon. He has the same thick-set body, square jaw clamped shut, eyes sunken and red-ringed. Tada follows her into the bathroom, looks at the blood falling like thick red petals on the white sink, gives a gasp like a plug letting out the last dregs of water and faints. He falls into her eight-year-old arms and she folds under him, her blood blobbing onto his blue pyjamas like ink on blotting paper.

Megan shivers and comes back to the present. She feels Ben brace her to him, a large, comforting hand on each shoulder before he slides his arms away and strides towards the front door. Megan blinks and watches Jim wake, hunched in the car. Her dad looks up and catches her eye, grins like a schoolboy caught on someone else's apple tree. He looks stiff as he gets out of the car, oddly unfamiliar in a patterned silk shirt.

Megan watches the men at the open door, Ben's rock-like calm easing the awkwardness. 'Hello, Jim, how are you keeping?'

'Not so bad, Ben.' Jim seems to affect nonchalance, but she notices he is shifting from foot to foot. He has that way of nodding almost without moving, Megan thinks, reconstructing him, that movement of the mouth that suggests a grin.

'Been here since four o'clock. I didn't want to wake you. Went to one of those workmen's caffs. Bloody awful! Put the kettle on, Megan, Cariad, there's a good girl.'

Megan says nothing. She blinks, turns back to the window to stare out past the empty car, past the blue July sky and into the past:

There is a place in Algeria, *In Salah El Golea*, which her mam insists is the root of all their problems. There is the desalination plant, which is for a time his unfamiliar home. The barracks, white blocks made out of the arid earth, shimmer in the molten glare of the sun. They know this from the photos, posted home by a friend of her dad. Her mam rails at them, furious when they don't answer back.

Her dad walks into the desert and out of the family.

There is the sick, sharp fear of not knowing where he is, what has happened, which gnaws and gnaws until the note arrives; a ten-word explosive inscribed on hair-thin paper tinted cloud-grey: 'Won't be home for Christmas, won't be coming home. Jim.'

Her mam wails and fumes, eventually exhausts herself in sobs. Then she rallies, a dervish from morning to night. In her fury she employs private eyes to track him down. The private eye traces him, but can do nothing else; no-one can bring him home.

Megan puts one foot in front of the other, determined with each step to move away from the crumbling cliff path of her childhood; a past as shifting as the dunes along Harlech beach where she used to play as a child on rare warm days; as shifting as the hot sands that her Dad walked out of in Algeria.

Megan tries to hang onto the story of her dad that she has rehearsed and recited in her head, year after year; the narrative that sanitises and contains the past, but the thread is broken now.

Megan rouses herself, but doesn't turn from the window. 'What's going on, Dad?' She doesn't face him. She stands, gazing out at his car.

'What you talking about, "what's going on?" I'm here, aren't I? Nothing going on, Cariad.'

Bombastic, her mother would call him, that and some other choice names, no doubt, Megan thinks.

'Nothing going on? You've been missing for eighteen months, Dad. Where have you been? What are you planning to do now?' She rounds on him, green eyes flashing, pale skin flushed almost to the colour of her magenta towelling dressing gown. He makes that familiar movement of his mouth: the half-grin. He holds out both hands and shrugs.

'Thought you'd sort that out for me, Cariad.' Again that grin. Did he do that to Nain to get his own way? Megan wonders.

'Give your mam a ring, there's a good girl, but put the kettle on first, Cariad, I'm parched for a decent cup of tea.'

Ben catches Megan's eye, opens comforting brown eyes wide: a silent question. Megan smiles back: *yes, go and get ready for work, I'm fine.* Ben exits upstairs.

Megan goes mechanically to the sink and turns on the tap. She is shocked at the gush of water, the ordinariness of how the kettle still retains its shape without melting into some other form in this suddenly strange world.

Jim makes himself comfortable on the red sofa. Megan watches him as he surveys the room, takes it all in. She reads his expression. She feels he approves.

'You want to go back to Mam?' Megan flicks the kettle switch, and turns towards him, incredulity in her voice.

'Well I'm not going anywhere else, am I?' He tries a small laugh, but chokes on it under Megan's astonished gaze.

'Er, sorry to interrupt, folks.' Ben reappears at the living room doorway in his suit. He looks towards the open plan kitchen to check that Megan is all right. He is grey and soft, Megan thinks, long-limbed and fluid. So unlike her square-chiselled, thick-set father. She has an urge to run across the room and cling to Ben, beg him not to leave her today, but she only smiles.

'Work calls,' Ben says tentatively. 'Michael Howard waits for no man.'

'Eh?' Jim jerks his jaw upwards in a question, body bristling and tense.

'Ben works for a Home Office department, Tada. He works in a project that gives funding to community schemes to bring down crime in poor neighbourhoods.'

'Sounds like a nancy job that, doesn't it? Thought Michael Howard was a Tory? Thought this clown you married was at least a socialist?' He waves his hand in Ben's direction, squat fingers punching the air.

Megan flashes a sympathetic look at Ben.

'Sorry, no time for all this stimulating conversation, folks.' Ben crosses the living room to the tiny kitchenette and kisses Megan lightly. He winks reassuringly, then he's out of the door with a 'See you sometime, Jim.' before Jim can reply.

Megan mixes milk and two heaped spoons of sugar into the tea, which Jim takes without thanks.

'Come on, Megan, no point bloody hanging around is there? Phone your mam, Cariad.' He sighs and sips his tea. Megan anticipates his thoughts: *Well at least it's not mud like that bloody caff tea, just some nancy taste that Ben likes, no doubt.*

'Tea okay, Dad?'

'Aye, well better than that muck at the caff, anyway. Bit of an odd taste to it mind, got a tang that reminds me...' He trails away and closes his eyes, opens them abruptly. 'You'd better get on with that call, hadn't you, Cariad?'

Jim watches Megan begin to dial before he closes his eyes to sip the Earl Grey.

I wonder what she is doing now, Consuela. She reminds me of Megan. Not in looks. Well, long hair: they both have long hair, I like that on a girl. Consuela's hair is shiny black, like a horse's coat when it's in good form, like oil on water, the way it ripples across a horse's flanks or down a girl's body. She's small, like Megan. And I suppose about the same age – no, she's more like Elin's age. "Fifty-five and twenty-five"– it sounds like a big difference when I think of it that way, but it didn't seem like it at first.

I'll never forget her. I can be there in a second; back at the first night we met.

I've had a few that night. I think Gary takes some photos: me and Ed and Ed's wife – what's she called? Bottle blond, mutton done up as lamb, everything on show: not what I like to see in a woman, but Ed's alright and it helps to oil the wheels a bit having a few of the wives out there, a bit of a laugh. It's not Cath's cup of tea, of course. Cath thinks I'm having a fling with whatever her name is – mutton woman. When I'm home she flings the photos Ed's given me round the room and shouts. 'I know what you've been up to with your blond piece. Sad old tart, don't suppose she's very choosy if she can stand to be anywhere near you!' Cath is drunk of course, and wrong. Never been near the woman, never been near any other woman in thirty-two years of marriage. I can't remember when I've last been near Cath for that matter.

Anyway, that night, there is Consuela, all of a sudden, standing at our table, clearing glasses onto a metal tray. She holds the tray at her waist, to one side, like one of those gypsy girls with flower baskets. She has one of those mouths that always seem to be smiling and lovely eyes: young eyes, with not the trace of a sneer. She has a good figure too, not bony like a model or especially tall, but good.

They have a lot of Asians on the site, domestics mainly or serving in the bar where the Mohammedans can't go. No Arabs are allowed in the compound because of the drink, so we have to have Asians to do the skivvying jobs there.

Mohammedans? I remember Megan telling me they don't call them that. She says something about that once when I'm home for a visit.

'Bloody Mohammedans,' I say, 'pray so much it's all you can do to get any work out of them.'

And Megan says, 'Not Mohammedans, Dad. They worship Allah, not Mohammed. They're Muslims.'

Megan is very up on all that, political correctness or whatever it's called. Anyway, they can't work in the bar so we have Asians there instead. But Consuela is different, all the way from the Philippines. What's the odds of that? Wouldn't back it for a bet, eh? Middle aged man from Blaenau, beautiful girl from Manila meet in a bar on some god-forsaken compound for the whites to live in while they're running a desalination plant in Algeria.

'It was meant', that's what my mam would say, 'It was meant'. I wonder if Mam would really say that, though?

She wouldn't like it, me walking out on Cath. She wouldn't take any excuses: the drinking and the screaming and the things that get broke when Cath hurls them at me, or all the years without so much as a peck on the cheek, but Megan might understand; she's always been my girl. I wonder what Consuela's doing now.

*

Megan watches her dad gulp down his tea, the way he wrinkles his nose at the scent of Ben's Earl Grey. She watches him close his eyes, slide off into his own world – always the dreamer. She dials the number carefully, but still slips a digit, has to start again.

'Mam? It's Megan.' Her voice is small and strangled.

'You're phoning early.'

'Yes, I've got some news.' She hesitates, glances at her dad. Jim takes a deep breath and blows, like someone in restless sleep. He half-opens his eyes and slurps noisily at the tea.

'It's Dad,' Megan says, her voice hardly more than a whisper.

'Oh yes? What about the bastard?' Megan hears Cath take a breath to prepare to launch into a full tirade against her missing husband, but she cuts in before Cath can begin the too familiar invective against men, blacks and the world at large.

'Dad's here, Mam. Dad's here at my house.'

'There? What do you mean there? What are you talking about Megan? Do you mean now? Do you mean the sly bastard's there at your house? With you? Now?'

'Yes.'

'Bloody typical.' The volume crescendos and Megan holds the receiver away from her ear. 'Bloody typical. He would come crawling back to *you* first, wouldn't he? It's always *you*, isn't it?'

'I didn't plan this, Mam. He wants to know if you'll see him.'

'Always you!' Her mother spits. 'What do you mean "see him"? I'll see him in hell, the stupid old git! It's always bloody *you*!'

'Mam!' Megan clutches the receiver and blinks hard, trying to concentrate on the present.

Megan is fifteen years old, curled on the nylon counterpane in the bedroom her dad has painted for her in the new house. The walls are yellow like buttercups. Megan cups her hands over her ears, but she can still hear the same tirade.

'It's always *you,* isn't it? You'd think it was you he was married to. I'm his bloody wife you know.'

Megan tastes the tears, sniffed back, sliding down her throat so that they almost choke her. Her mother looms over the bed.

'First it was his precious mam, now it's you. I'm his bloody wife. Not you, not her. Me!'

'Mam, listen...' Megan blinks harder, tells herself to concentrate, '...perhaps you should meet somewhere neutral.' Megan continually brushes a strand of hair from where it falls into her eyes. 'You're going to need some marriage counselling at the very least, Mam. You don't have to rush into anything.'

'What the hell do you know about married life?' her mother says. 'Shite to counselling! Tell him to sodding well get himself to your sister's house right now. I'll give him pissing about going to you first, he wants to remember who he's married to. You've got Elin's address?'

'Of course, Mam. I...'

'Hang on,' Cath cuts in. At the other end of the line Megan can hear a muffled argument before her mother resumes.

'Elin doesn't want him here. She's got more sense. So I'll come to you. We'll sort this out at your place and then the bastard can take me home. We'll stay at yours tonight, drive to Wales tomorrow. We'll have to see what sort of state the house is in; you know how the damp gets in when it's empty. How long does it take from you to Elin? An hour or so? Elin'll drive me, but she won't come in, not till he's got himself sorted out.'

Megan puts down the receiver. It's not yet nine o'clock in the morning and she longs to curl up small back in bed.

'Looks like it's going to be a nice day out, Cariad.' Jim nods towards the window. He shifts uneasily on the plush fabric of the red sofa. Megan understands he

17

wants to ask her what Cath said, but he'll wait: *Megan will tell me whatever I need to know.* She predicts his thoughts wearily.

'Yes, Dad, it does look nice.'

'Always liked July. It was the end of May when we had you and we had a lovely June and July that year. Lovely having a little baby in the summer.

'Elin was born in July, Dad.'

'Of course, but then you were the first, Megan.'

'You remember it's her birthday tomorrow, don't you?'

'Whose birthday?'

'Elin, Dad. She's twenty-four tomorrow, July the seventeenth.'

Megan brushes a hand through her hair and bites on her lip as she observes her father.

'Well, your mam'll have something for her. I'll be here for your thirtieth, though, eh?'

'Dad, Mam is going to come here. She'll be about an hour or more. I have to get dressed and go out, but I'll be back before Mam's here.'

'Out? What do you have to go out for? If you want something from the shop I could nip there or drive you. Might as well make myself useful while I'm here.'

'No, it's just round the corner, Dad, I've got an appointment.'

Jim frowns and his dark eyebrows meet across his leathery brow. 'You're not ill? You look alright, might even have put a bit of weight on, not that you couldn't use a bit of weight.'

'I'm fine, Dad, I'm…we're…Ben and me are going to have a baby – at the beginning of January.'

'A baby?'

'Yes.'

'But Megan, you're…I mean…'

Megan turns away, reminds herself to breathe into the silence.

'You know what your mam went through with you and Elin,' Jim falters, 'It's just…a baby…another baby…"

'Another baby, Dad?'

'What?'

'You said "another baby". I haven't got another baby, this is the first and it's a long time since me and Elin were babies, Dad.'

'Yes.'

'Are you okay? You look…well, you look a bit green around the gills.'

'Just got up too early this morning, Cariad. You'd better get ready for your appointment, eh? Got a paper I can read? Not to worry, I've got one in the car – expect Ben'll only have some snotty English rag.'

'Last night's *Guardian*, Dad.' Megan attempts a smile. She recognises he won't be led – that he's already changed the subject.

'Leave the door on the latch if you go out to the car for your paper, Dad. I'm going to get a shower.'

Megan walks upstairs slowly, as though testing every step for solidity. She turns the thermostat up on the shower, loses herself in the steam and succour of the hot water, drenches herself in the thick, comforting smell of honey and ylang ylang shower gel. Her tiny bathroom is white, calm and reliable, her bedroom blue and tranquil. She dresses carefully for the ante-natal appointment: sensible cotton underwear, clean white t-shirt, loose cotton-print skirt – though there's still not much to call a bulge.

Downstairs, she pops her head around the door, red hair still damp, held by a blue velvet band. 'I'll be back soon. Make yourself more tea if you like.'

She knows he won't stir on his own behalf. When she was seventeen and going out with Ben he always waited up, hovering around anxiously until she came home. Then he would fuss around, pour her milk, offer to make a bacon sandwich, knowing she would always decline. Sometimes he'd make one for himself, or put the kettle on and make tea.

It was the only time he ever did anything for himself.

'Bye, Cariad.'

A baby? In January? At the same time? I'll be a Granddad. Me a Taid and a…Who was I kidding? Turning fifty-five and being told *that* by a girl younger than Megan. I couldn't take it in at first. Then it was like being hit with a cold wave on Cardigan Bay, the sea slapping the air out of you. I've never felt so old. Fifty-five: it's a hell of an age to think you can start all over again, especially in a place like that.

It's not like the movies, not really: sun on your back, silk shirts, a good looking girl who doesn't resent every little thing. Paradise? Maybe. But maybe I'm not cut out for paradise. It was bound to end sooner or later, but when she told me that, on the day of my fifty-fifth birthday, it was all over. The ultimate present, she said, but I could see the worry in her eyes before she opened her mouth.

'Are you pleased, Jim?' Consuela was flushed, her eyes blinking back fear.

'Yes.'

What else could I say?

Another baby and all I can do is sit here and wait for Cath to come and scream the place down, take me home, throw whatever comes to hand: insults, ornaments, furniture.

I wish I could start it all again. I'm tired of all the misery.

Only Once

In Salah El Golea: I can't tell them what that place was like, not even Megan.

They tried to give us an idea of what it would be like – acclimatisation they called it, all lectures and glossy leaflets. But it's never like the pictures, is it? There are hills all along the coast, the 'Tell' they call it; hills with mountains behind them, higher than the Moelwyns. It took me a while just to say the name of the place. I couldn't say most of the names, it was like trying to talk with a mouthful of treacle. The names are foreign, they grate like the soft sand carried on hard wind that gets into your skin: Grande Kabylie, Bejaïa Plain, Soummam River. Not that you get to see much outside the compound except the odd excursion with the lads. I got some sand roses and a scorpion in a paperweight on one of those trips, brought them home for Megan. Wonder if she has them still?

The soil's not much good in most places, except round Algiers and apparently that was just malarial swamp till the French did something to clean it up – managed to plant vineyards and lemon trees. Typical French, get wine out of a stone, but fair play to them. Anyway, most of the place was too dry even for them: scrappy little farm villages picking a living out of not very much.

The desert, the real Sahara, was a lot further south than the compound, but we had the odd trip. It makes the dunes at Harlech look like nothing, that's for certain. Ergs they call them, fifteen foot or more, some of them. Further out it's not all sand, there are plateaus and mountains, but we never went that far. Somewhere out in the middle is a massive plateau where the Berbers live, the Mzab, and after that the Sahara is bone dry, hardly an oasis to be seen – only the nomads and the oil camp workers go there, tough bastards the lot of them.

They called it temperate where we were, on the coast. 'A mild Mediterranean climate' the leaflet said. What they didn't tell us is that every valley and hill has its own weather and some years are completely different. It never gets cold; it's broiling in summer, twenty-four degrees, more in the warehouse. It's more like spring in the winter, but always humid. You never feel clean, you're covered in sweat five minutes after a shower.

They told us we wouldn't get the wind, the Sirocco, but it felt like we got it to me; sand dust blowing off the desert like glass teeth sometimes, so Christ alone knows what it felt like right down there in the Sahara. In the summer the air is leaden – like carrying hot bricks on your back. I missed the rain. I missed the greyness and those greens in autumn that look soaked to softness. Soft in the head, I suppose.

The plant is run by Yanks of course, but most of the blokes are Brits, a few Jerries. The Algies can't run the place for themselves. They'd had a revolution against the French, then different governments, different regimes. Now they're Islamic Socialists. Fair play to them, I'd say, but apparently they can't organize much.

In Salah El Golea sounds like a girl's name, some high class, exotic film star, but the compound isn't high class. It is white blocks covered in dust next to the plant that hums day and night, like some enormous fan whirring our lives away, grinding out every minute of boring, mind-numbing work, every second of every long, lonely night. The plant is nothing special, just another industrial plant – more modern than the hydro-electric power station at Tanygrisiau, and much bigger. The air smells of salt instead of coal. I miss the smell of coal...

I hate early shifts, getting up bleary eyed before five in the morning, inching my feet onto the freezing floorboards of the bedroom to tiptoe out without waking anyone, feeling like I'm the only person awake in the cold and dark.

When Megan is a baby I walk the floor at night to soothe her. When she falls asleep I inch her into the cot next to our bed, then fall asleep in seconds between Megan and Cath. Never more than three hours before I have to stumble up again, freezing cold in the unheated bedroom in winter, pull on some clothes without waking the pair of them and shuffle downstairs for a quick cup of tea before the off.

When the mines were open we lived by sirens, but in Algeria it's prayer. Not that they are always that religious, but it's their way. They talk about being less Western, some of them, about some group with a French name that's going to win the elections and make them all proper Mohammedans again, or Muslims or whatever they call themselves. I've never set much store by religion. I tried chapel once or twice when Mam died, but it didn't do anything really. Religion is just another way to kill each other, I think.

They'll be at it over here soon, butchering each other like they do in Ireland, where Cath's mam comes from. Anyway, there's the prayer, but it's not the same time every day; it shifts around. It's got something to do with the moon, some kind of calendar that has to be worked out every day. It keeps the priests in business, the mullahs or muezzins or whatever they call themselves. Five times a day. Bloody piercing. Eerie, if you ask me, and some of them really go over the top with it. The boy who works under me in the stores is one of them, facing the right way or Allah won't accept his prayers, making a fuss about no-one walking in front of him or he'll have to fight them, then all that droning. 'Insha Allah', everything is *Insha Allah* – can't do a thing otherwise. It makes the hairs on my neck stand on end, but I suppose it makes me think.

It makes me think of my mam: 'What will be, will be' she always said. And: 'It'll happen if it's meant to happen'. Not a lot of difference when you think about it: *Insha Allah*, 'if it's meant'. That's how things are everywhere: prayer times or fate or buzzers – different ways of letting you know that life isn't in your own hands. When it comes down to it I imagine that's what most people think, but I can't explain that, not even to Megan.

Megan thinks she makes her own mind up, she thinks she lives her own life, but I know it's not like that.

It's different out here, it's different, but it's the same: you do what you have to, whether you're here or there. At home, I have to go to work, I have to put up with Cath, I have to do my bit, until there is no work and I have to leave. Out here, I have to be with Consuela; it's my last chance. No one like her will walk into my life again.

I walk out of the bar and there she is, looking up at the sky. I saw her earlier; watched her clearing glasses. She watched me watching her, picked up each glass slowly, hardly glancing at what she was doing. She's small, maybe a bit taller than Megan, but not all bones like Megan. She's Asian, but not like the moon-faced girl in the Chinese takeaway. Her hair is shiny and almost black. It moves in one long piece, as though it's weighted.

'Think you're in there, mate.' Gary nudges me, leers, and that spoils it. I look away, swill down more beer to cover my face. Bloody Gary! Any idiot can see she's not like that. She finishes clearing the glasses and walks away. Gary whistles after her, arsehole that he is. I have half a mind to go after her, say something stupid like: 'Don't mind him, it's just the drink talking' or something completely soft in the head like: 'He's just someone I drink with, not a real mate – you take what you can get out here'. Not that I have that kind of nerve. But she doesn't take any notice of Gary. I'm pleased about that.

So there she is when we come out, first Ed and his wife, leaning on him, legless as usual, pitching forward on her heels so that her bust hangs out of the thin top that's too small for her: common as muck, not like Consuela. Then Gary, laughing at one of his own jokes, his camera strung round his neck. I let them get ahead of me, wave them off.

'See you in the morning.'

I hope they'll just stumble off without saying anything, but Gary has to turn round. 'Nice one!' He winks and nods towards Consuela. I want to wipe that silly smirk off his face, but I ignore it, wait for him to go away.

'I like to look at the sky before I sleep. I think how I share the same sky with the people at home so it doesn't seem so far away,' she says.

I don't say anything back, just look up at the stars.

'You don't want to know where home is?'

I nod again. She laughs then, a bit nervous and it hits me that she's not much more than a kid, but I stand there anyway.

'You are not a man to say much, I think. My home is in the Philippines. You know about it?'

I shake my head.

'You are English?'

'Welsh.'

'He speaks!' The laugh again. Maybe she's taking the Mickey or maybe it's just nerves. 'You look dark for Welsh. More Spanish, yes more like that, but you are Welsh?' She says the word carefully.

I nod again.

'Well, Welsh, you like the stars?'

'Never really thought about them much.' I look up anyway.

'No!' She laughs again, teasing now, getting into her stride. 'You cannot say this. You are silent like the stars. I cannot believe you do not think about them.'

I think, I have never had a conversation like this. She lifts her face to the sky again and is quiet. The half light from the high slit windows of the bar behind us catches her long hair, and I can just about make out the shadowed face that she holds up.

'Perhaps, I will see you tomorrow, Welsh.'

She moves to walk away, back to her room on the compound.

I begin to watch her go.

'Excuse me.' Excuse me? For pity's sake. Is that the best you can come up with: 'excuse me'? She smiles as she turns, a teasing smile still, but patient. 'I wonder...if you don't mind, I wonder if you'd tell me your name.'

'Of course, Welsh. My name is Consuela.'

Consuela. I want to be back in my room so that I can say it out loud. I've never heard a name like it; it makes me think of her laugh. It's a name like a long drink – Consuela. Soft, like Megan – the name I insisted on when Cath had wanted to choose something clipped and ugly: Janet or Tracey, one of those names that Cath said were modern. Consuela: the name curves like her body.

'So Welsh, you won't tell me your name now?'

'Jim.' It sounds flat and ordinary. 'Short for James,' I try to make it more appealing, something rounder and more dignified. 'Like James Stewart.' I add.

She tilts her head on one side. 'James Stewart?' She has a slow, amused voice. When she speaks the sounds seem to lengthen in her mouth. 'This is one of your English kings, I think?'

'No, well, yes, there was a James, at least one, or maybe two, but we don't go in much for English kings in North Wales. I meant the actor, Jimmy Stewart, he's my favourite. Do you like films?'

'Films.' Words sound different when she says them, light and young like her voice. I could be in a film right now, some unreachable actress making words sound like ice cream melting on her tongue.

'Films, you know – Movies. Do you like movies?'

'I love movies, Jim. Movies make you talk to me.' She winks, I think she winks, and walks away, slowly. She turns back, briefly before she rounds the corner of the bar, a hand half raised. 'Good night, Jim.'

I stand there, dumb-struck. Was that something or nothing?

The stars don't answer. The night cold is seeping through my thin cotton shirt. 'Good night, Consuela.' I say it out loud to the stars, to feel the taste of her name in my mouth. This is something, I tell myself.

The Philippines. I don't even know where that is. Somewhere in the sea near India, I think. When she shows me on a map it's further over than that – way out in the ocean, off the coasts of Vietnam and China, but not close to either of them. Underneath Japan. Right out in the ocean. I've always liked the sea.

It's not really like a country, more a group of islands, a big one at the top and then others, some bigger, some smaller.

'I'm from Baguio, up here in the mountains.' Her hair falls across the map when she points, longer even than Megan's, but straight and dark like a horse's mane. 'It's cooler in the mountains and the best vegetables grow there and strawberries that everyone should taste.'

I smile back at her. Mountains cool enough to grow strawberries doesn't sound like the mountains I know, the Moelwyns, Snowdonia. Megan loves strawberries, but I can't talk to her about my daughter. Instead I smile like an idiot and watch her dark hair brushing against the map that is laid out on her white bed in a plain white room like all the others on the compound.

'I moved to Manila when I was twenty, and cleaned house for a family who worked for Kellogg's. We have lots of American companies in Manila. They told me about working here in Algeria for good money. We are both here for the work, Jim.'

She puts her head on one side when she smiles, looks like she's asking a question.

'Suppose we are. There's no work in Blaenau anymore. Mind you there's plenty of Algies that don't have work from what I hear, but they can't run the plant like we can.'

It exhausts me, all this talk. I can listen to her all day, but I think she expects me to say something now and then. I don't say the Algies can't do the bar jobs because of their religion or that the Asians seem to do all the cleaning and skivvying jobs. She knows all that, anyway.

So here I am and here is Consuela.

I wouldn't do it at home. I'd look, the way all men look, but that's all. I'm fifty-three, been with Cath since I was twenty, married at twenty-one. Thirty-two years is a long time married and I'm past the stage of thinking things will ever get better; given up that hope years ago, even me, the dreamer. It is a different place here. Out here I'm not a bloody fool or a washed-up has-been told he's good for nothing. Out here I'm a man with a bit of money, a good job by their standards: warehouse foreman, not just the lackey. Out here being Welsh is something special and being fifty-three gives me a bit of clout instead of making me over the hill and past it. Out here I'm someone who can look at stars and think about things. Out here I'm Jim, a person grabbing the last chance I'll ever get.

Consuela. Consuela is like nothing I've ever known. She looks at me, doesn't just glance. Consuela is not ashamed – of her body, of what she wants. Not ashamed to look me in the eye. I can't shake this feeling that I'm in a film. She has this look, like she's

30

taking a long, deep breath of me: salt, grit and all, the way we breathe in sand and salt in this place. She takes me in and still looks at me as though I'm something. She takes her time. She is twenty-three. She has all the time in the world.

'I can't imagine what you see in me at my age.'

'At your age? What is this age that makes someone not be seen?' She laughs at me, leans back and gazes at me, sees me.

I've never seen eyes so dark.

'You know what I mean. You're a young girl.'

'At my age, Jim, I want someone real.'

Megan has lovely eyes: green, sharp, and questioning, never misses a trick, but in Consuela's dark eyes it's like I'm reflected back, no questions. I am someone I want to be.

'So salty.' When her tongue flicks over me every nerve ending judders. I never get over the shock of her, even though she's so slow, and delicate with it. I can't think of ever feeling so fragile, like some thin piece of nearly transparent best china licked clean. She closes her eyes, as though she's filing every flavour of me away, as though I'm not just sagging skin and aging fat.

She breathes in so slowly I start to wonder if she'll ever breathe out again. I hold my breath myself. When she has finished ingraining her body with the scent and taste of mine, she steps back, unfastens the tiny white silk robe and drops it to the floor.

She smiles and stretches out on the narrow bed.

My hands are full of her; nothing has ever been so soft in my hands. She smells of sun and desert winds: spicy, salty and sweet. It is every night now. We pretend it is in secret, but everyone knows and we don't really care, not out here. We stay together all night, always in her room, floating between drowsing and sleep, blatant and shameless. She is soft and brown and never says no. Sometimes we go out into the darkness to watch the stars. Sometimes we hear the first call to prayer in that time before morning and I think of the sirens and walking the floor with Megan until she would finally fall asleep in my arms.

I wonder if I am the same person. Maybe the dreamer has gone too far this time, but what can I do? I think about Cath, of course I think about her. When Consuela is asleep I gaze at the two crumpled photos I have of Cath: the one of Cath as a kid, all grinning teeth and crumpled socks in a school photo she kept, barely eleven and the spit of Megan at that age. The other on our wedding day, me grinning fit to bust, Cath looking gorgeous and proud outside the chapel.

I gaze at Consuela asleep, at the pictures of Cath: one Cath before I knew her, one Cath who I can hardly remember knowing, and I can't remember which life is real.

Escape

Holyhead County School, 1950

In the photo Cath is smiling. She is fourth from the left, on the back row. She has no idea why she is smiling, standing there with thirty-three other girls who smell, like her, of cigarette smoke, overcrowded homes oozing body odours and boiled tripe. They are the class of 1950, class 1b. She is eleven years old, almost twelve, already broadening and developing unwanted signs of womanhood. Cath stands and smiles and lets her mind wander.

She has been back from the Children's Home for nearly two years now, but she still thinks of it every day: the neat little beds, the enormous rocking horse at the end of the dormitory, no Mam constantly calling on her:

'Cath, see to that baby's nappy.'

'Cath, put the kettle on.'

'Cath, mind the kids while I nip out for a couple of hours.'

'Cath, do you want a good lacing?' Like a lacing is some delicate feminine ritual.

These crwt are not her real brother and sister, except for the baby. Her and Nest are the real children and Dad thinks so too. He hates the others more than she does. Cath crinkles her nose for a second, thinking of the tall, fair American.

'Hey mister, can you sling my rope over the lamppost for me? Will you?'

'Sure thing.' He takes the end and reaches up with it.

33

He looks at Cath, head on one side, uncombed red hair, plump, full lips that grin under the palest eyes; grey flecked with green.

'Would you be Cath?'

Cath opens her mouth without sound.

'Your Ma told me all about you. And this would be Nest?'

Nest hangs back, blushing and gawping.

'You those kid's dad?' Cath demands, jabbing a hand towards the house. Her mother is cooped in there with the two children that were there to surprise them when they returned from the Children's Home.

'I surely am and I can be yours too if you'd like. How'd you like to live with me and your Ma in the States?'

Cath pictures her mother the day the letter arrives, crying over Wayne who will never send for them now. His family regret to inform Mrs Elinor Parry that their only son, Mr Wayne Larson of Illamoak, Oregon died tragically in a diving accident.

The bends. Cath turns the word over until it sounds strange and alien. She holds her big fixed smile for the second camera flash.

'You have to have a man, Cariad,' her mam says over and over after she stops crying over the letter from America. 'Better the devil you know...'

So Dad saunters back in one day, like he's never been away, like the American was never there, like Cath and Nest hadn't just spent three years in a children's home while their unfit parents beat each other with fists and taunts till one went to war and the other found a replacement. Dad's all smiles for at least half an hour.

'You'd better keep your filthy brats quiet if you know what's good for you.'

'I expect my tea's not on the table because you're too busy hanging round the marine yard, slattern.'

Mam doesn't answer back. Instead, Mam has a way of making Dad think about something else. Cath watches her mam work her dad up till he explodes, smacking a kid or finding some other grim amusement to take his mind off his wife. Mam's wiles don't work all the time though. Cath hears them through the thin bedroom walls: the slaps and the grunting, pig noises. She huddles down further into the bed she shares with Nest, tries not to smell the fear and the piss from the bed with the kids in it across the room. Cath watches her mam swell with the new cwrt, her dad's only son. Owain is one of the real kids, like her and Nest. Dad's got a boy now, but it only makes him hate the other kids more.

Dad hates Patrick most. He will be five at Christmas; he gets the worst of taking Dad's mind off Mam. He howls at the sight of the belt and wets the bed at night so that Cath has laundry to do every morning before school, before she gets the kids' breakfasts. Anita is two, always snotty and smelling of piss. Cath hates her most, with her stuck-up American name and blonde hair like the Yank's, but Dad ignores Anita most of the time.

Cath distantly registers the last flash of the camera.

'That will be all, girls.' Cath hears Miss Evans's voice, far off and all syrup in front of the school photographer. Cath turns off her smile and follows the line of girls back to her classroom to finish another afternoon of fear.

'Cath Parry, what did I say?' Cath stares like a rabbit caught in headlights, forces her hands onto the desk, palms down, as Miss Lowry approaches, ruler raised for the strike.

'Cath Parry, you are a dull...' The slice through the air, the first crack of pain. '...insolent girl.' Cath holds still; a reaction will only make things worse. 'You will write 100 times, "I must pay attention in class". Do you hear?' The last biting rap.

'Yes, Miss Evans.'

Next to her, Mannon Jones smiles, a thin flick of scorn. Cath retreats back into her head. She has no idea about answers. She lives from one punishment to the next, the rest a blur of daydreams or fear. At home at least her dad has Patrick to thrash, though she hates having to listen. Sometimes, though, Patrick isn't enough, sometimes it's her and Nest too: a good lacing, her dad calls it. It's not good, but it's not as bad as the other thing...the thing that she can't let herself think about that.

'Cath Parry! You are still not listening to a word I say. Stand up girl! Walk to the front!'

Cath walks slowly, every eye in the classroom focussed intently on her. She can taste the dry mix of chalk and fear on the still air where every breath is held in; she can feel the class tremble with expectancy, almost excitement. Cath stops in front of Miss Evans – dull brown eyes, thin tight lips, a sharp nose that curls away from the smell of unwashed girls. Cath's pale face flushes, she stands in front of Miss Evans, grey-green eyes already plump with moisture. She gazes at her scuffed black shoes and holds herself still.

'Hold out your hand.'

At the sound of the wheels on the gravel drive, Cath glances up through the kitchen window of the Druid's Hospital. She sees Jim notice her, blushes and ducks her head down, hoping the girl who works alongside her in the hospital kitchen won't notice. She concentrates hard on washing the potatoes in the ice cold water that makes her hands swollen and blotched.

'You going to the dance next Friday?' Mary has blonde curls and red lips. She winks. She winks so often that it might be an affliction.

'I'm going to the pictures with Jim,' Cath says quietly.

'Thought you liked to dance?'

'Jim doesn't like dancing.'

Jim is serious and quiet, a sign of intelligence, Cath decides. Jim is deep, that's what they say: still waters run deep.

'You're over Jacques then?'

'He's gone home.'

'Didn't know they had Jews in France. Couldn't marry one though, could you?'

Cath runs her mind over Jacques: dark, like Jim, his eyes almost black, but a face like a sculpture, all delicate bones, not at all like Jim. Jacques said he wanted to marry her. He said he would take her back to France. She scrapes the peeler roughly across a cold, lumpy potato and wishes she hadn't told Mary about Jacques. France indeed!

She thinks of Mr and Mrs Cohen still, their precise kindness that let her know her place: Their house is clean and quiet, the kitchen has two sinks, two of everything so that everything can be washed separately:

meat and dairy. Something to do with their religion. When she washes the wrong dishes in the wrong sink Mrs Cohen throws out the muddled dishes, as though nothing can ever make than clean again. Cath wonders if they will tell her to leave, but Mrs Cohen smiles and explains again, in her quiet, sympathetic voice.

Jacques, the son of a cousin or some distant relative, bursts into the Cohen's tranquillity. He is not kind. He does not let Cath stay in her place. He makes her blush. He makes her think about those places on her body that she never looks at. When Jacques takes her dancing Cath allows Nest to use her black eyeliner pencil to draw lines on the back of her curvy legs. Afterwards, she wriggles into one of Nest's pencil tight skirts. She twists her body against the mirror and blushes.

'Does it look French, Nest?'

'Of course it does.'

Mr and Mrs Cohen send Jacques home. They don't ask her to leave, but they look at her with such sadness, such disappointment. Cath applies for a post in the kitchen at the TB hospital. She asks Mrs Cohen in a whisper if she could be so kind as to give her a reference, please.

Jim never tries to slide his hand around her body. He never looks at her as though he can see through her prim clothes, as though to suggest that a girl as curvy as her must be less proper than she appears. Jim doesn't dance, but he loves the films. He takes Cath to see everything showing. He loves them all, the old black and whites and the new shiny colour flicks full of glamour.

They sit in the middle of the cinema, where decent people sit, swathed in smoke. They peer longingly at

Bergman and Bogart and hold their breath as their screen idols deny their grainy passion for the sake of duty. They gape at the wide open spaces of frontier America and admire the stubborn goodness of James Stewart in *The Man from Laramie*. Jim adores the women. He tells Cath he imagines himself as the lead man, Bogart or Cary Grant, but most of all James Stewart.

Cath smiles into the cold water where the potatoes float amongst muddy bits of peel. How like James Stewart Jim is. Not many words, but there's something good about him. Jim is always clean: crisp white shirts, thin dark ties and a good navy jacket. His hair is almost black and always in place, Brylcreemed flat and shiny.

After the third date, Jim takes Cath home to show her off to his mother.

Sarah looks Cath over with piercing blue eyes. 'I know a mother shouldn't say it, but Jim's my favourite. Don't know why.' She looks at Jim with a mixture of puzzlement and tenderness. 'He's not tough like his big brother Hugh and he's not smart like his little brother Alun, but I've always had a soft spot for him, daft as he is. He's told you what a pen dafad he is?'

Cath gulps and smiles thinly. She tries to hold her cup the way Mary at work says is the proper way and winces as tea sloshes into her white china saucer.

'When did you say you would be eighteen, Cath?'

Cath begins to say that she had never mentioned her age, but stops herself.

'August.'

'And what do your parents think about you marrying my Jim?'

Cath sprays fine droplets of tea into the air and feels her colour rise impossibly.

'He has asked you to marry him, hasn't he?'

Jim shrugs and makes a familiar movement of his mouth towards both women, the sheepish appeal that he learnt as a small boy.

'Well, I'm sure I don't know what we're going to do with him, Cath, really I don't.' Sarah discretely passes Cath a starched serviette to wipe the spray of tea from her face. 'But you'll marry him all the same, I suppose. He has a way of getting his own way. Now then, tell me all about yourself. You have a lot of brothers and sisters, don't you? Your family aren't Catholic?'

Cath feels her face, burning still. 'My mam, my mam was brought up Catholic, but not my dad.'

'Irish?'

Cath nods.

'But they didn't bring you up like that? You don't want a Catholic wedding?'

Cath shakes her head.

'Well that's good enough for me.'

'You like children?'

Cath blanches. She thinks of saying 'maybe one day', but says nothing in case Sarah guesses that she is lying. She's had her fill of children, of nappies and snot and endless washing. She wants to curl up in Jim's arms and sleep for a long time at the mere thought of children. She has no taste for doing what is needed to become pregnant. She wants to be safe and looked after, not mauled and pestered.

She blinks under Sarah's steady patient gaze.

Sarah smiles generously. 'Well, I'm sure in time, no doubt. You must have had a lot of practice with little ones. Jim loves children. He's so good with Carri, his little sister. She's four – dotes on Jim.'

'My little brother Tom is four.' Cath grasps at the thread of conversation.

'Is he the youngest?'

'No, I've got a sister who's two, she's called Sian.' Cath colours again. 'And another baby due in September.'

Her mind flashes with hatred towards her embarrassing mam with all of her flaunted bodily functions. Here she is trying to appear suitable to Jim's mother and she has to confess that her mam, at the age of thirty-eight, when decent people might be expected to know better, has no self-control.

Sarah smiles again, but it reminds Cath of the same rueful smile that Mrs Cohen had. 'Your mother must be a very busy lady, Cath.'

Cath nods. She doesn't say that most people wouldn't think so, that most people know that she and Nest bring up all those flea-bitten crwt, pleading with them to keep quiet; to not tear their shoddy clothes; to not come home covered in mud; while Elinor Parry sits in her chair whining at the world and goading her husband.

'Where does your father work, Cath?'

'The Marine Yard.'

Sarah nods. 'Jim, that's Jim's dad I mean, worked on the railway before we had the shop. Would you like more tea?'

'Please.' Cath moves the bone china towards the matching teapot.

The front room is no bigger than the Parry's front room, but Jim's parents own this house. It's not rented and there is a big three-piece suite in bottle-green leatherette. They have a long kitchen, scrubbed clean and with tidy cupboards and another room with a big dark table and dark pictures in thick gilt frames on the wall, a room that is only used on special occasions, at Christmas or for funerals.

Jim's parents buy good cuts of meat for Sundays and eat fish and chips on Fridays, not tripe and onions, bread and jam, bread and dripping and rarely, humped-backed pies. Cath looks into her tea and blinks back the scene she left at home this morning.

'Look at this place! Just look at it, Slattern!' Dad has her mam by the hair, parading her around the kitchen. Mam has a stained brushed cotton nightdress on underneath her loosely-tied beige candlewick dressing gown. Her full, sagging breasts show through the gap in the front. Her pregnant belly strains at the greying fabric.

'Tell them lazy so-and-sos,' Elinor spits back. 'I'm six months gone and do they lift a hand?'

Nest and Cath exchange furtive looks and bite their tongues. Patrick and Anita huddle by the back door, eyes flushed with panic. Tom, undoubtedly Dad's son in looks and temperament, and his only son now that Owain has gone, pinches Sian hard so that she squeals, breaking the tension.

Dad lunges for Sian, pins her flailing, scrawny body across the kitchen table, lifts the toddler's flimsy dress and smacks hard, while little Tom sidles towards Patrick and quietly begins to squeeze another lump of flesh. Patrick flicks Tom away a little too robustly and then freezes, aware too late that the eyes of everyone except the sobbing heap of Sian are now turned on him.

The belt makes its familiar thwack as it leaves its anchorage around Dad's thick middle. Cath catches her

42

breath, inhales the sour odour of unwashed children sweating fear and closes her eyes for a moment. She hears Patrick's slight weight roughly hit the kitchen table, opens her eyes to watch little Tom grin as Patrick's worn trousers are pulled down for extra effect.

Elinor sighs as the thin, shiny fabric rips. 'More mending!'

Cath and Nest simultaneously lift hands over their mouths, blink in unison to force back the tears. Patrick is crying before the first welt takes him across his thinly veiled behind and exposed thighs. Anita shrinks further down between the back door and pantry, choking back her sobs with a grubby fist wedged into her mouth.

When he's finished, Dad glowers around the room.

'Anyone else want a taste of this?' He flicks the belt menacingly against his hand. 'Well then, stop making a mess! It upsets your mam. Can't you see she's got enough to do?'

Elinor almost purrs until she catches the glance exchanged from Cath to Nest.

'Look at that!'

'What now?' It's Saturday and Dad is wearying of this sport. He should be down the club by now.

'Those two dirty madams. Lazy as you like. Swan around this place like two lady mucks. Out all hours with their fancy men they are, and stand there giving me filthy looks, if you please.'

Nest lets out the slightest gasp of protest or terror; enough to single her out.

Dad walks around the bulky, scratched table that takes up most of the kitchen, lumbers towards the big chipped enamel sink that Nest and Cath are backed against. He pushes his whole weight against Nest, his face red, his breath sour, the words slow.

'I'll deal with you when I get home.'

'But I'm going...'

He doesn't raise his voice, simply pushes in closer so that Nest can hardly breathe. 'But nothing, madam. You will be upstairs waiting for me when I get home, not out with that waster Tony, as if I didn't know what he's after, you dirty little tramp. Now get upstairs and wait for me.'

He backs up a fraction at a time.

'The rest of you will do as your mother says and if I hear one complaint when I get back I'll give every one of you the hiding of your life.'

He casts a final leer towards Nest and Cath. 'And don't think any of you are too big for it,' he adds with a final flick of his belt before he re-adjusts his sagging trousers and lazily rethreads the weapon.

Cath fingers Sarah's bone china cup. At home they squabble for the cups, thick green cups with tannin infested cracks and stained chips. The losers get jam jars to drink out of, the stewed, milky tea slurping unevenly over the thick ridged rims of the glass. Cath puts down her cup delicately and smiles. She is going to marry Jim. She is going to escape the shame of being a Parry to become a Vaughan.

Sarah smiles back.

December 1956

In the photo Cath is smiling. Jim is wearing a black suit, thin lapels, drainpipe trousers. Cath wears a suit too, thick and blue, warm for December, practical so that she can use it again after the wedding. She clings to Jim's arm under the grey chapel archway and smiles. The photographer is a grey, stooped man with one eye that wanders off sideways into another reality. Behind him the crowd rub their arms and stamp away the cold or warm, their hands around lighted cigarettes.

Cath scans the faces with her fixed smile. Nest looks thin and sick. The boy she's courting stands too close to her and glowers at the world with his dull, thuggish face. Patrick is even thinner, his straight pale hair and blue eyes single him out. At least Anita had the good sense have Mam's eyes. At eleven, Patrick reminds Cath more and more of the American: tall, pale, fine-boned and gangling. There are no visible bruises on Patrick. Dad is careful about that, but Cath watches the stiffness in the way he moves.

She thinks of that night, the worst night, when he answered back. 'You're not my real dad, anyway. My dad was a man. My dad was an American hero.'

She fears for him now that she is not in the house, but Patrick won't do that again. She still hears the screams in her sleep; Patrick's animal howls.

Cath screws up her eyes against the winter sun and readjusts her smile.

'Lovely, Mrs Vaughan.' The squinting photographer encourages her, 'that's just right.'

Anita hangs onto Patrick's hand, her nine-year-old nose dripping in the cold, her ingrained grey socks hanging limply around her ankles, but there is a glint of defiance in her dark eyes. There is no Owain. Cath glances across the churchyard to the neat white headstone, glinting with slime green moss in the cold winter sun. .

On either side of her mother, the little ones are whining. Tom has dark curls and eyes as dark as Dad's – at four, Tom already has the sneer of being the 'only real son'. He tugs on his mother's dress with one hand, pinches his two-year-old sister with the other. Sian kicks back at Tom's shin and Dad instantly scoops her up, legs flailing in the cold December air, one arm bracing her slight body in a tight lock. He swings his free hand hard against her behind as she hangs from his arm. Sian starts to cry on the third slap and Dad slaps her again as a warning, before he sets her down. Cath watches her mother's face. Elinor clucks and shushes at Sian and shakes herself free of Tom's clinging hand.

Without breaking rhythm, she rocks the baby, swaddled against the biting cold: another unwanted girl. Cath flushes, embarrassed by the spectacle of her ragged family: Elinor, still bloated from the last pregnancy: her breasts pendulous inside the cheap print cotton dress, bouncing as she rocks baby Bron. Cath flushes deeper, ashamed, and crosses her arms. Further off, Jim's family stand together, neat and quiet. Two brothers and two sisters, each a sleek, dark copy of their quiet father. His mother smiles, smart in a dark green wool suit neatly finished with a string of pearls.

'That'll be it, Mr and Mrs Vaughan,' the photographer says through his fixed smile. He pulls himself upright from the cumbersome camera and rubs his back. 'Thank you for your patience ladies and gentlemen.'

Cath turns off her smile and follows Jim down the chapel path away from the Parry's. She is Mrs Vaughan now. Dad will never touch her again.

Enough

It is already ten past ten. Megan sighs. She would like to walk along the old dockside through the park, enjoy the warmth of the July sun on her skin, sip juice sitting on the glass and steel balconied café overlooking the new waterfall at the dockside shopping mall. She places a protective hand over the baby who has hardly made a bulge yet and sets her face towards home.

Elin's car turns into the end of the street as Megan rounds the corner. A fat BMW, pale as a maggot. Her dad bought the car the last time he was home. Was it nearly two years ago? Megan watches her sister pull in behind her dad's hire car. Elin has red hair like Megan. Thicker, darker, straighter and cropped short, but red. They have the same green eyes, but Elin's eyes are dull, she looks exhausted, and Megan can imagine why. Megan wonders how she would cope with Cath's demanding, unrelenting presence in her home. Elin doesn't smile. Elin never smiles, not since she was a little girl pulling the heads off dolls, taking everything in her path apart and laughing uproariously. Not since before she went to school.

Megan goes to Elin's door and pulls it open. She leans in and kisses her sister's cheek. 'Hi Elin.'

'Hi Megan.' Elin screws up her face.

'Headache?'

Elin nods and Megan wonders if the headaches ever cease.

Does Elin have them even when she is not with her family or does she secretly revert to the sunny, easy-going girl that Megan remembers.

'Come in. Take something for it and have a drink.'

'No thanks, Megan. I've got to be getting back, Terry's expecting me at the office.'

Megan smoothes her sister's expensively cropped hair. 'Are you sure, Elin?' Elin nods, lips pursed, the tension in her shoulders visible.

'Okay, but make sure you drive carefully. Are you doing anything tomorrow?'

Elin shrugs as Cath steps out of the other side of the car. Her faded red hair is pulled back tightly around her hollow face, which is twisted into its usual sour smile.

'Don't bother to say "Hello" to me, Megan. I wouldn't want you to put yourself out or anything...'

Megan stifles a sigh. 'Hello, Mam.'

'Ben at home?'

'No, he's at work.'

'Good. We don't need him poking his nose in our family business.'

Megan wrinkles her nose at Elin, who shrugs again. Cath slams the car door shut and walks to the pavement. She doesn't thank Elin; she doesn't say goodbye.

'My bag's in the back of the car, Megan.'

'I'll get that, it's heavy.' Elin swings out of her seat.

'Oh, don't make such a fuss, Elin, she's not the first person in the world to have a baby. Where your father's been they have their babies in fields, just squat down like animals in the paddy fields. It won't hurt Megan to carry a bag.'

Elin moves round to the boot without replying, opens it and lifts out the bulging suitcase. She lumbers its weight to Megan's doorstep and steps back. 'I won't come in, Megan,' she reiterates.

'Okay, but I'll ring you later, see how your headache is. You take care of yourself and have a good birthday. Terry's got our present. Look after yourself.'

'I will.'

Elin's voice is small and strangled. She retreats to the car and Cath pushes past the suitcase into the house.

'You'll need to get that case for Lady Muck who can't carry anything,' Cath says to Jim by way of greeting. She turns towards Megan, who is hovering, breathing in the mounting tension.

'Well, put the kettle on, Megan. You can manage that even in your condition, can't you? Always did say there was more go in half a scissor.'

Megan edges across the room and begins to make tea. From the corner of her vision, she watches her father stand mute and uncertain.

'What are you dithering about, man? Fetch the bloody case in.'

Jim moves, galvanised, and Cath slumps into the place Jim has hollowed out for himself on the sofa. The case takes up the whole hallway and Jim has to manoeuvre around it to close the front door. Back in the living room, he stands awkward and silent until Cath barks at him. He takes up the seat opposite the red sofa, a chair wedged under the stairwell, and perches on its edge.

'So what have you got to say for yourself?' Cath begins.

Jim shrugs.

'Is that it? Is that all I get after what you've put me through, you shite-arsed bastard?'

'Mam!'

'Shut up and make the tea, Megan. This has nothing to do with you.'

Megan thinks of a hundred replies, but bites her tongue. She will lie awake for nights to come thinking of this, how it could have been different, but the exhausted resignation that she'd seen in Elin's eyes is already creeping into her bones. She wonders why her dad had come back.

'Anyway, why aren't you at work today?'

'I work from home on Mondays, Mam, I...'

'Very nice for some and they call that work?' The sourness of Cath's mouth has set so hard that her chin seems to be entirely separate, like a jointed ventriloquist's dummy.

I edit manuscripts here because it's quieter, no interruptions, Megan continues in her head, and I do call it work, actually.

Megan pours two cups of Earl Grey and wishes Ben had some PG Tips tucked away at the back of the cupboard.

'Maybe you'd like some time alone?' Megan offers, handing out cups that she and Ben bought on their last holiday in Devon: chunky hand thrown bowl shapes with swirling blue and terracotta glazes.

'Funny bloody cups, these,' Cath says. 'You can sit down and keep quiet. You'll only be bloody earsdropping anyway.'

Eavesdropping, Megan corrects silently, and what do you want me here for if I'm supposed to keep out of it? But she keeps her peace and settles herself on the far end of the sofa.

'I know where you've been.'

Jim glances up, wide-eyed, but doesn't reply.

'I'm not daft you know. We have bloody private detectives in this country; it's not like some third world hole where they know shite all.'

Megan winces, but joins her father in keeping the pained silence.

'So, what're you crawling back here for? Money run out or has your fancy whore got someone else now? Woke up one morning and realised what a sad old git she was crawling into bed with?'

'Mam!'

'Don't "Mam" me. So what was she like, your little tart? Long hair? About Megan's age?'

Megan shudders and folds her arms around herself.

'That's enough,' Jim says, his voice a thin rasp, but edged with determination. 'There's no need for that.'

'Really? So what're you doing here then? She's not your bloody mother, you know, your mother's dead and spinning in her grave, I'll bet. And she's not your wife either – I'm your bloody wife! You forgot that a long time ago though, didn't you? Long before you lowered yourself to screwing black tarts. Well, didn't you?'

'I said "that's enough".'

'And I say it isn't. I haven't even started yet!'

Jim's face is flushed. Cath fixes her mouth into a hard leer, contempt flicking over lips that have thinned with age and bitterness.

Megan's skin prickles. 'This isn't getting you anywhere,' she says quietly. 'Mam, you said earlier that you wanted Dad to take you home, back to Wales. Is that what you want?' Megan wonders why she keeps on being drawn in, but the pattern between them is too familiar to abandon now.

Cath glowers. 'Don't you start throwing my words back in my face.'

'I'm not throwing anything at you,' Megan persists. 'I'll go away if you like, but if you want me here I presume it's for more than just hearing you shout abuse. I only wondered if that was a place to start: that you want Dad back?'

'He is back.'

'He's here, yes, but you can still decide what to do.'

'I'm his bloody wife. What else can I do?'

'So you want Dad to go home with you?'

'That's what I said isn't it?' Cath is petulant now. She looks sunk and hollowed-out, Megan notices: thin and anaemic, in contrast to her plump and sun-baked Dad.

'Right, so you both want to be together. Is that right, Dad?'

Jim shrugs, manages a plaintive smile. Megan glances from one parent to another.

'What else can I do?' Megan hears her mother saying.

Megan thinks of saying something insightful about the habit of hate and self-loathing that magnetises the pair, but she only sighs.

'I don't know how you can look me in the bloody face!' Cath shouts. Her voice is caustic, but there is a hint of tears.

'Don't think I won't give you what for when we get home.'

Megan watches Jim hunch down in the chair. She closes her eyes and hears the same words from twenty-four years ago: I'll give him what for when he gets home, don't you think I won't.

Megan is five years old. She watches her mother from the kitchen door. At five, she knows all the signs. The words splutter, ranting faster and faster in time to the eggs and bacon sputtering in the frying pan on top of the gas stove.

'Shall I draw you a picture?' Megan offers soothingly as she backs towards the dark wood dining table in the cramped living room.

'What bloody good would that do?' Cath retorts without turning from the pan. She gives the pan a furious shake, tips in a tin of tomatoes that let out a gasp at that heat, then shakes the pan harder.

'Tada won't be long.'

'Tada won't be bloody standing upright if he doesn't get his arse in here in the next minute.' Cath lunges for the grease-covered knob on the front of the stove, twists it into the off position and gazes at the pan of fried food. 'Bloody ruined.'

There is a tiny pause, a tense silence before Cath slowly lifts the pan into the air. Megan watches her mother turn. She always moves slowly, bloated with the baby that has inflated her like a red-faced, monstrous balloon. Cath balances the pan for a moment, holding it above her enormous belly with both hands. She breathes in and hurls the pan across the room, towards the door where Megan is hovering. Cath lumbers after the pan as Megan scurries for cover under the table. Her mother can't bend, can't even tie her own shoes. From her retreat, Megan watches her mother kick the pan around the living room. The bacon lies limp by the kitchen door, the egg yolk is spattered on the door frame, the tomato makes a long angry trail from the kitchen to the living room fire place.

Along the route Cath encounters Megan's doll, a rag doll the size of a toddler: print cotton dress, long yellow wool hair, a brittle, smiling face in moulded plastic. Cath glances towards the table. Under the shadow of the cloth she can just make out Megan's skinny shape. Cath picks up the doll and Megan hears a small choking noise, Mam swallowing down tears. Cath drops the doll and stamps hard on its face. The crack of the plastic is like a giant beetle breaking. Megan lets out one stifled sob, chokes back the rest. Sally! Sally, her baby. The baby that Nain gave her. Megan buries her face in her hands and curls up small.

The door opens a few seconds later.

'Home, Love.' Jim pauses at the door from the passage. He takes in the pan, the food smeared like entrails across the carpet, the doll with its face split, globs of white and blue stuffing leaking out.

'Where's Megan?'

'Oh that's right! Think about Megan. You're bloody late. Your dinner's bloody ruined. I stand here seven months gone, cooking like a bloody slave just to let it all go to waste because you can't be arsed to get yourself home on time.'

'The bus was late, Love.'

'Don't you bloody "Love" me. What do you bloody care about me? Come waltzing in here with all this,' Cath casts a defeated hand over the mess, 'and all you bloody care about is "where is Megan?". Under the sodding table, that's where.'

Jim crouches next to the table, lifts the checked cloth that hangs half way to the floor.

'Come on out, Cariad.'

Cath sinks onto the black leatherette settee that divides the room into eating and living space, cramped too close to the open fire.

'That's right, make a fuss of her. Don't mind me.'

'She's just a kid, Cath.'

Megan shuffles out towards her tada, glances towards Sally.

'Don't worry, Cariad, I'll get some tape for her head.' He picks Sally up from behind the settee, flicks away a smear of tinned plum tomato. 'Look, it's up the top, Cariad. If I tape her up and we get her a little hat she'll be good as new.'

Megan nods.

Cath watches the two of them through narrowed eyes. 'Just a bloody kid, my arse. She's all you bloody care about. I'm your bloody wife!'

'Course you are, Love. I'll put the kettle on and get a cloth.'

Cath lunges for the pan beside the fire place, but her belly has no give in it and she can't bend. Without the pan to throw she reaches instead for an ornament from the mantelpiece, a china dog with a screwed up face, and launches it towards Jim. Megan retreats to the sanctuary under the table again and pulls Sally in from where she lands when her tada drops the doll as the dog catches him on the shoulder. She watches the china shards rain down beyond her small, safe enclave and curls up again, hugging Sally to her. Megan tries not to hear what follows, the escalating insults from her mother, the tired denials from her father, the crash of ornaments in flight.

In a lull, she peers out. Cath is on the sofa, her face beetroot. She is rocking, holding herself and rocking back and forth, red and swollen. Jim stands, back to the fire, mute.

Megan creeps out, goes into the kitchen and fetches a clean tea towel. 'Dry your eyes, Mam.' Cath stops rocking and takes the cloth. She dabs at her face obediently, sinks back further into the sofa and sniffs.

'Go and make some tea, Tada,' Megan says quietly. Jim stirs and walks towards the kitchen. Megan follows him and goes to the sink for the dishcloth, a wet, grey square of loosely woven cotton. In the living room she begins picking up pieces of food, carrying the cloth back and forth to the kitchen bin, standing on the little stool to rinse it in the sink, starting again.

'There's a good girl,' Dad says in whisper, glancing nervously into the living room where Cath is quiet now. Megan follows his glance, nods in reply.

'Of course he's coming home, Megan, before he finds some other little tart to shack up with,' Cath spits out, turning towards Megan.

Megan pulls her mind to the present. 'Well that's a start, Mam. So you're going home and then what?'

Cath and Jim speak at the same time:

'Then I'll give him hell.'

'Then we just get on with things.'

'Do you really think revenge is a good reason for being together, Mam?'

'It'll do me,' Cath says acerbically, 'he can't just come waltzing back in and not pay for what he's done.'

Jim puts his head into his hands and sighs.

'Don't you look so bloody hard done by, you big useless lump.'

'Mam!'

Cath is in full tirade now. 'Who the bloody hell was she? Some black prostitute that needed a meal ticket? Must have seen you coming! Filthy little whore! Bet she was full of diseases. A black, for Christ's sake, could have been anywhere, probably drops everything for any white man with a fiver.'

'Enough.' Jim stands, clenches both fists in the air, sinks back down into the chair. 'There's no need for that,' he says through gritted teeth, 'I'm home, aren't I? Let's just leave it.'

Cath's laugh is scornful. Megan winces at the contempt that oozes from her sour, down-turned mouth. 'You must be joking. You come home on my terms and I'll say what I bloody want and if I ever catch you trying to write or phone or so much as thinking about the filthy bitch, I swear I'll knife you as soon as look at you.'

'I said I'm home and I'm home, that's that.'

Bedrooms

December 1965

The bedroom at Nain Parry's house smells of damp. For a moment Megan wonders where she is. The peeling wallpaper with its blotches of blousy roses looks dizzyingly unfamiliar.

She smells the musty scent of stale urine, feels the slippery surface of the mock-satin eiderdown thrown over the heavy pile of blankets and remembers: they often stay here when Mam needs a break from Tada. Sometimes Aunty Nest comes too, when Uncle Tony is bad. The bed smells because of her cousin, Gethin, who is six, more than a year older than her, but he still wets the bed. Megan isn't sure what's wrong with Uncle Tony, she thinks they should be looking after him if he's bad, at least getting a doctor out to him, but instead Aunty Nest leaves him alone and cries a lot.

Cousin Gethin isn't here today, but Aunty Sian, who is eleven, and Aunty Bron, who is nine, are both asleep beside her. In their sleep their faces look almost identical. Megan squints at them, puzzling them apart in an effort to wake up. Sian's tangled hair is darker, thicker than Bron's matted wispy hair, which has a red cast when the light falls in a certain way. In the other double bed, next to her mother, is Aunty Anita. She has hair fair like Uncle Patrick and dark eyes that always seem to Megan to be laughing, except when she's crying over something Taid Parry has done to her. Mam has red hair, like her own. Megan's hair is longer and brighter, but Mam's is just as curly.

Aunty Anita and Mam are propped on a pile of pillows, the thin scratchy ones with feathers that poke through, leaning on their elbows, Anita stifling giggles.

'You're such a scream, Cath.'

'It's nothing to laugh about. I mean it. I've got enough with one brat. I never wanted kids at all, but this one's definitely the last.' Mam puts a hand over her belly and glares up at Anita. 'I had my belly full of kids with you lot round me neck when I was here.'

'Ah, Cath, it's different when they're your own. And you've done alright. She's a nice kid, your Megan, bless. Bit skinny and gawky looking, but she's bright as a button.'

'She's that alright. Any sharper and she'd cut herself. All babies are is shitty nappies and sleepless nights. I won't be spoiling this one. He was a pain in the arse when Megan was a baby – "Don't put brandy on her gums, Cath", "Has the baby been changed, Cath?", "Don't leave her cryin', Cath." This one will do as it's told right from the start. And I meant it: that's the last time he'll get a chance to leave me like this.'

'But, don't you have to?'

'Who's going to make me?'

'Won't Jim get...?'

'Get what? All he'll do is sulk. He wouldn't dare lift a finger to me and he wouldn't dare look elsewhere, either. I'd have his precious Megan off him faster than he can blink, and he knows it.'

'But won't you miss it?'

'Miss what?'

'You know.' Anita rolls on the bed giggling.

'You're joking!'

'I would.' Anita props herself on the pillows again. Her dark eyes look shiny and excited.

59

'What?'

'I'd miss it.'

'Anita Parry, you should wash your mouth out. Who've you been skulking round with? You stupid girl. It's dirty, you know, you'll catch something if you're not careful.'

'I already did.' Anita smirks, sits up and rubs her belly.

'What?'

'I've fallen for one too.' Anita grins.

'A baby? For God sake, Anita, you're seventeen, the old man will kill you!'

'Will you tell Mam for me, Cath? Please.'

Megan sits up in bed and stares across at Aunty Anita.

'How long have you been ears-dropping for?' Cath catches Anita's eye. 'Told you she's a sly one.'

Megan yawns and rubs her eyes. 'Are we at Nain Parry's?' she asks, innocent and bemused.

'She's alright, Cath.' Anita throws back the sludge coloured shiny eiderdown and holds her arms out to Megan. 'Come here, Meggy, I'll take you down for some breakfast. Do you want hot milk on your cornflakes?'

Blaenau Ffestiniog, June 1966

The bedroom at Nain's house smells of cough sweets, polish and disinfectant. The quilt on the top of the bed is dark red and gold and the room is panelled in the same dark wood as the wardrobes and chest of drawers. Underneath the bedroom is the shop where Nain and Taid used to sell sweets. Megan closes her eyes and imagines the shelves of glass bottles, some glistening with jewel coloured sweets in thin sticky cellophane, others full of dark toffees or the hot brown bullets of cough sweets that Taid Parry sucks on endlessly. The shop is a junk shop now, full of dust and old furniture.

Megan wonders where her tada is and then remembers that he must be at work, six-till-two. They sleep here when he has to get up early. When he's on the late shift she goes to the lady down the road. The lady is called Gwen, but Tada says to call her Aunty Gwen.

Aunty Gwen has two cats, a fat ginger one with a clawed ear and a scruffy black and white one that tries to sit on Megan's small, bony knees and knead her with his little needled paws. Aunty Gwen has a boy called Dafydd, who is exactly one day younger than Megan. Dafydd always gets red faced trying to tell Megan that he's the oldest because he's bigger than her. Sometimes he sits on Megan to prove it, his fair freckled face going redder and redder like he was standing too close to the fire and his blue eyes almost crying as he shouts, 'I'm the oldest!' over and over until Aunty Gwen pulls him off and threatens to tan his hide.

Megan waits quietly at Aunty Gwen's house till Tada fetches her. Aunty Gwen always offers Megan something to eat, but the house smells strange and Megan says she doesn't eat fish fingers. Aunty Gwen ruffles Megan's hair so that coils of red stick out fuzzily around her sagging pony tail band, 'You're a one-off, Megan Vaughan.'

Aunty Gwen says this whenever Megan refuses food. Megan smiles at her and doesn't ask what being a "one-off" means, though she plays the phrase over in her mind.

When Tada comes for her he carries her home in his arms, all the way down the street and Megan sleeps in her cot next to Tada's bed. Nain bought her the cot when she was a baby. It is painted white with metal runners and a blue rabbit on the inside of the headboard. The line round his floppy ears is peeling slightly. She has slept in this cot for five years now.

Last week Megan had chicken pox and Tada stayed home with her. He bought her new colouring books and new crayons and said they were a present from Mam in hospital, but Megan knows he made that up. Now that Megan is feeling better, Tada has gone back to work and she is waking up at Nain's house, lying in the big comfortable bed.

Megan hears someone making their way down the long upstairs passage: Nain, or maybe it's Carri, her aunty who is fourteen.

'Morning, sleepy head.' Carri is tall and skinny with long brown hair and a short red mini-skirt. 'Come and get dressed, Megan.'

Carri holds out a new dress that Nain bought for her. It has a big white collar, a full skirt and little puff sleeves – a proper little girl's dress, Nain says, tutting over the lime-green nylon crocheted smock that shows Megan's petticoat through the open stitching.

'After breakfast, I'll take your picture with my new camera. Mam says we can go out on the roof, but you have to be really careful. You won't go near the edge, will you?'

Megan finishes pulling on her vest and nods seriously.

'Good girl. You can take a picture of me, too. I'll show you how. I might be a model one day.'

Megan wriggles skinny arms into her petticoat, then the dress, and lifts up her newly cut red hair. Tada had her hair cut because he couldn't get the tangles out while Mam is in hospital. Megan hates it. She's not speaking to Tada, even though he bought her a lovely Snow White watch to say sorry.

'It's so fine, Megan,' Carri says, running her fingers through Megan's sleep-tousled hair, 'It was a terrible tangle before, you know. It's gorgeous like this. You wait till you see the pictures, you look a real little cherub.'

Megan shakes her head as Carri reaches for a brush, but she thinks perhaps she might like the pictures and she might be nice to Tada again when he comes to fetch her later. Megan settles in front of Carri and closes her eyes. She likes this bedroom best, especially the big wardrobe that is cluttered with Nain's fur coats, boxes of costume jewellery, stiff nylon petticoats, layer upon layer, and glittery dresses from long ago when Nanna says she could dance a Charleston or the ones left behind by Tada's big sister, Aunty Menna, when she became a married lady.

Blaenau Ffestiniog, July 17th 1966

Tada takes Megan upstairs to the bedroom she has known since she was born. It is at the front of their poky Victorian terrace, with the noise of buses always rattling the windows and the smells of fusty sleep in the cramped air. The alcoves on either side of the fireplace hold a matching wardrobe and chest of drawers: bulky, shiny walnut pieces that Nain had bought. The double bed has a green headboard in a material that Mam calls velour with a purring, pleased tone. The baby is in the bedroom, wrapped tight in a soft, crocheted blanket and fast asleep in Megan's cot.

'Megan, this is your sister. We're going to call her Elin Angharad.'

'It's in my bed.'

Jim laughs, sits on the double bed and lifts Megan onto his lap. 'You've got a new bed from Nain's house. It's coming today. Uncle Alun's going to bring it over in his van later.'

Megan wrinkles her nose. Uncle Alun, who is younger and taller than Tada, sells wet fish that reminds her of the urine-scented bed at Nain Parry's house. 'Will it smell?'

'Of course it won't smell, Cariad.'

'Where will it go?'

'Right here. We can move Mam and Tada's bed right over to the wall, then your bed, then Elin's cot.'

'Does it just stay asleep all the time?'

'Elin? No. Some babies do sleep a lot, not that you ever did, but they don't sleep all the time.'

'You don't have to pick it up, though?'

'What do you mean, Cariad?'

'That baby, you don't have to pick it up, do you? I'll be yours and the baby can have Mam.'

Jim laughs nervously and hugs Megan to him, strokes his daughter's silky hair. 'Don't you worry your head about it, Cariad.'

The bedroom in the new house is small, but has more light. Her narrow bed runs the whole length of the wall and there is no room for a wardrobe. Instead Tada puts a chest of drawers on the landing outside her room. Megan retreats to her new room as much as possible, avoiding the long, sullen silences and dangerous rows that flare unpredictably. Next to her bed is a tiny child's chair with a seat woven in pink and green nylon. Nain said it was made by unfortunate people at a home that looks out to sea, right next to the beach, but it doesn't smell of salt and wind, only of cigarette smoke, like the rest of the house. The lamp that stands on the chair also came from Nain. 'Another cast off,' Mam says, the same as Megan's heavy bed with its metal frame and dark wood headboard that she has had since Elin was born more than three years ago.

At night Megan listens to her tada out on the landing, pacing like a zoo animal, sobbing: a horrible dry sound that makes her own breath catch in her throat. She falls asleep to the rasping sound, then wakes, squashed and disoriented. It is still dark. She is not alone. She begins to twist and her father holds her still, one hand stroking her hair.

'Shh, good girl, it's only me.' Tada starts to weep – real tears, a torrent unlocked from dry, red, sleepless eyes. 'Good girl.' He buries his face in her hair, sniffs back a sob. 'Don't say anything, Cariad, not to anyone.'

Megan listens to the tears subside, shivers and wonders if Tada is feeling better now.

Egbert's Estate, Tanygrisiau, 1976

At Lewis's furniture shop on the High Street in Blaenau, they choose together, Dad and Megan. The wardrobe and dressing table are not like the old things handed down from Nain, they have a fragile look; the light wood finish is glued on to clean white melamine and the handles are plastic, made to look like gold metal. The new bedroom is painted yellow with a yellow carpet, tufted, her mother calls it, and a yellow nylon bedspread that is edged with a sheer curtain of transparent yellow fabric, scratchy and full of static.

'So you won't need a valance,' her mother comments, though Megan doesn't know what a valance is.

The yellow bedroom is at the front of the house overlooking the field towards the new road in the distance. The curtains are yellow. It smells of incense from the new Siop Werdd, full of lentils and beans that are dry and in packets. Her Mam turns her nose up, but Megan is fascinated.

'Stinking the place out,' Cath comments, lighting her cigarette.

When the yellow room is finished, Dad sits on the bed and gazes into space. 'Well, I'm off tomorrow, Megan.'

'Yes.'

'You'll look after your Mam, won't you?'

'Yes.'

'You'll be alright, Cariad.'

'Yes.'

'Is that all you're going to say to me, then?'

Megan laughs. 'Yes.'

He stands up and hugs her to him. She squirms away, but smiles. 'Will you write?'

'Doubt it, Cariad. I wouldn't know what to put.'

Megan tilts her head to one side, amused, long red hair falling in a thick plait. 'Okay, well, see you in three months, then.'

'I expect so.'

Cath pushes open the door. 'Might have known you'd be in here.'

'Just saying good-bye, Love.'

'You can do that tomorrow. Anyway, you're only gone five minutes, more's the pity. Your bloody tea's going cold on the table.'

Megan watches her parents leave the room and sits on the yellow bed. Mam is already planning their next move 'out of this council house dump' that she blames Tada for them 'ending up in'. Tada can't get much quieter, here or in Algeria. He's not just quiet, though, more morose, more distant than ever since being made redundant the last time. Elin calls Jim 'Stig of the Dump' after the caveman in the book Megan reads aloud to Elin at bedtime – the caveman who only grunts.

After Tada has gone to Algeria Cath starts coming into Megan's room late at night. The yellow drains into grey shadows in the streetlight beyond the thin Crimplene curtains so that Megan can only dimly see her mam's outline. Megan breathes evenly, feigns sleep, squints at her mother without fully opening her eyes. Her mam stands over her, silent, shoulders heaving. 'I'm his bloody wife,' she hisses each night before leaving. One night Megan thinks that mam raises her arm high, something glints in the muted light; something like a knife. Megan squeezes herself tight.

She feels a cold lick of fear making a puddle of sweat on her back, but she stays silent, holding her breath, flattening herself soundlessly into the mattress. Mam lowers her arm. 'I'm his bloody wife,' she says.

Megan wonders next morning if she dreamt the knife, but after that night Cath doesn't come into the yellow bedroom again. She leaves Megan's clean clothes or bedding on the landing outside her door and one day there is a new petticoat: cream cotton edged in two layers of lace – a long hippy petticoat that Megan has coveted for months and her mother has turned her nose up at.

'I just thought you'd like it,' Cath says gruffly, arms folded tight against any thought that Megan might hug her in thanks. 'No need to make a fuss.' Cath rapidly leaves the living-room to put the kettle on. Megan returns to her yellow bedroom, arranges the cream petticoat on her yellow bed, and cries into its lacy folds.

London, July 16th 1990

Megan makes a quick detour from the bathroom to her calm blue bedroom, the bedroom she shares with Ben. The pale pine furniture catches the sun, warm and uncomplicated. The quilt over the duvet is patchwork, liberty prints and Laura Ashley florals hand-stitched by Megan. Megan sinks onto the pine framed bed, breathes in the quilt, scented with lavender essential oils, and runs a hand over her still flat, but pregnant tummy. She inhales deeply and opens her eyes to scan the world she has made for herself and Ben: shelves of books, novels and poetry, her favourite volume of e.e. cummings lying open on the desk where she edits manuscripts on the days when she works from home, on the walls two pen and ink sketches of a women seated in a wicker chair by an attic window, herself as a student drawn by Ben, and a Moroccan wall hanging in deep and pale blues.

From downstairs Megan hears Cath's impatient call: 'Are you bloody coming or what, Megan?'

Cath's footsteps shake the stairs and she stands in the doorway. 'Bit bloody insipid this room, isn't it? You want to cheer it up a bit, Megan.'

If Only

In the living room Jim closes his eyes. He hears Cath and Megan moving upstairs and sighs deeply.

What a mess.

The first time I see Cath, she's sitting on a bench outside St Bride's with a gaggle of girls from the TB hospital's kitchen where she works. It's autumn, one of those cold days when the leaves are blowing down like gold rain and the sky is so blue it makes your eyes water to look. It must be 1955. Jimmy Stewart is making great movies: *The Far Country* and *Rear Window* last year, and I've just seen *Strategic Air Command.* There she is. She has the most stunning red hair; I've never seen anyone with hair that colour. She has it tied back in one of those high-up pony tails, masses of it swinging down her back in wild, silky curls. She is wearing a blue skirt that hugs her hips and a pale blue blouse that follows her shape. She's a really great shape. I sit at the wheel of my ambulance for a moment, and think: I'll take that girl to the pictures, to The Palace to see *The Man from Laramie.* Then it comes to me: I'm going to marry that girl.

I keep an eye out for a moment when she is on her own, not surrounded by the giggling kitchen girls, most with mousy hair and flat, shapeless bodies and the blonde one who's too pushy for her own good. I wait around in the long windowless Victorian corridor with its shiny lino floor smelling of disinfectant. I can stand in the shadow and watch the kitchen door from here. I snatch my moment when the girl whose name I don't know yet, but who I know I'm going to marry, goes to the store room for bags of carrots.

'Hello there, I'm Jim. James, like Jimmy Stewart. You like Jimmy Stewart?'

'I suppose so.' The girl crosses her arms in front and takes a step back.

'I thought you might like to go to the pictures with me.'

'Did you?' She has green eyes, sea green with flashes of silver like moving waves. I like the sharp little challenge in her voice, but it almost ties my tongue in a knot till Jimmy Stewart comes to my rescue.

'Aw shucks, ah shoo' did,' I drawl in my best Jimmy Stewart voice, hang my head and shrug.

She laughs. 'Alright Jim,' she hesitates and I think she's going to change her mind, but she lets her arms swing down and nods, more to herself than to me, 'you're on.'

'I am?' I want to hug her straight away out of sheer gratitude.

Instead I steady my voice. 'I don't know your name.'

'Cath.'

'Cath, I like that.'

'You do?'

'Of course, it's kind of…well Catherine sounds like a name from the movies.'

'Catherine Mary Parry.'

She has an incredible smile, incredible lips.

'Catherine Mary Parry.' I say it out loud. It feels round in my mouth like some soft fruit. 'That's beautiful. Pleased to meet you Catherine Mary Parry. I'm Edwin James Vaughan. The third, or maybe more than that, it's one of those family names – we're always called Jim.'

I'm babbling now and she looks cool and amused.

'So, the pictures?'

'Saturday night. Where do you live?'

Cath folds her arms again, purses her lips. 'I'll meet you. Where are you from?'

'Blaenau Ffestiniog, but I'm at my brother's in Bangor to be near work.'

'The Palace?'

'Yes.'

We set a time and a place to meet and I walk away on air. Catherine Mary Parry is going to be Catherine Mary Vaughan. I just know it.

After we've seen a couple of movies I tell my mam that I've found the girl I'm going to marry and I'm going to bring her home. Cath's from Holyhead, but she stays over with an aunt in Llangefni for work. She's a bit quiet about her family, I can't quite get all her brothers and sisters straight in my mind for a while, but I manage to get her talking about one of the little boys, the one that died earlier this year from some kind of blood poisoning. Cath says they told her it was from eating mud pies in the garden that another little brother had made.

'Tom must've given the baby, that's Sian, some of the muck too, but maybe not much because she pulled through,' Cath says. 'But Owain, well he didn't make it.'

'That's a shame. I don't like to think of little kids in pain. Doesn't seem right, does it? And the others are alright?'

'None of the others were sick, just Owain and Sian. Of course Patrick and Anita are old enough to know

72

not to eat muck, but so was Owain really. Tom's only little, but he wasn't sick at all.'

'Tom's the one the same age as Carri?'

Cath nods. 'He's four.'

'She's a real sweetie, Carri. You'll love her. I play with her for hours. Must be great to have all those little ones around, eh?'

Cath puts her head on one side and looks at me. 'Are you sure you want to take me home?'

'Of course I do, Mam'll love you.'

Mam won't mind about Holyhead, I think, she's not uppity like that. 'Always give people a fair chance', that's Mam's motto.

I'm right about Mam: she likes Cath's quiet voice and the way she colours easily. Cath's not like those girls Hugh used to bring home before he settled down with Margaret. Mam likes the way Cath appreciates everything and she likes that Cath makes me happy. That's good enough for Mam.

We're married by the next December, four months after Cath's eighteenth birthday, with me coming up to twenty-two. We live in a flat in Criccieth: two rooms and our own little bathroom at the top of a big house overlooking the sea. Cath has a job in a real kitchen at a big hotel. She's a silver service waitress and she loves it. She loves everything clean and how shiny the silver cutlery has to be. Our flat is as clean as the hotel kitchen. You could eat your dinner off Cath's floors.

I have a new job too, at the Oakley pit. It's a long haul on the train from Criccieth, but I'm never late for work like some of the lads.

I think one day I'll have a little farm with a big, clean kitchen for Cath and lots of children, at least four, maybe five like Mam had, with one coming along late like our Carri, cute and spoiled, but not really spoiled. The farm will be like my Uncle Alun's farm out beyond Llan Ffestiniog, with pigs and sheep and a pony for the children.

Cath loves to clean, but she doesn't like to cook so much. Still, we get by. I can get a meal in the canteen at work and there's always corned beef in for sandwiches. Anyway, I can do a good fry up or beans on toast. I can manage with the food, but the other thing bothers me. Catherine Mary Vaughan, it's such a full name, all curves and colour, but only by name, not by nature. Cath doesn't even like me looking at her.

It's hardly any wonder that it takes more than four years before she falls for a baby, the way she slaps my hand away, won't put up with so much as a kiss most of the time. Cath sleeps in a thick brushed cotton nightdress. She has a way of getting into it so that nothing shows. I sometimes wonder if she knows herself what her own body looks like.

We have to move out of the flat when Cath is finally expecting. Children aren't allowed, although the landlady says she'll make an exception for us. Mrs Prichard likes the way Cath keeps the flat so clean and that we're quiet, but Cath is worried about the baby making a noise.

'You're so daft, Jim, babies cry all the time you know.'

'Not all the time, Cariad. I'm sure our baby won't and Mrs Prichard is two floors down most of the time. I thought you liked it here. And we can afford this.'

'Mrs Prichard's not two floors down at night. That's when babies do most of their squalling. You wanted this baby, now you'll have to find the money for a bigger place.' Cath's eyes flash warning shots of green and grey and I know she's sick a lot with the baby, so I try to make allowances.

'Of course I want the baby, Cariad. I couldn't be happier. You're pleased too, aren't you? We'll be our own proper little family and if you think we need to move, we'll find somewhere. I'll have a word with Mam. Don't you fret about anything, Cariad.'

I try to hug Cath, but she crosses her arms in that way she has, tenses so that it's like trying to hug bricks. I smile instead. I'll start looking for a place, make sure Cath has nothing to worry about. She's only thinking about what's best for the baby.

My mam's so pleased about the baby, especially after all this time when she was beginning to think there was a problem. Of course Mam doesn't know that Cath just doesn't like that kind of thing and it's not something I can tell her. Mam says she'll help with the deposit for the landlord and furniture and that we won't have to worry and we find a place on the High Street in Blaenau.

'It's a bit busy with the buses going up and down,' Cath says when I take her to see the house. She wipes her finger over the outside window ledge and grimaces at the black on her finger tip. 'Filthy.'

'We'll soon have everything spick and span, Cariad. Mam'll give us a hand and our Menna said she'll help us get settled in. There's a back yard and it's not like the baby'll ever get near the buses and traffic, and it's handy for getting to work.'

Cath looks unconvinced, but I put it down to the sickness with the baby and with worry. She's bound to worry more with a little one to think about, it's only right.

I prattle on, trying to calm Cath, 'And there's the shops really close so you won't have to walk far if you need a few bits.'

Cath sighs and looks tired. My mam gives us old furniture as well as the deposit. There's a double bed, a table and chairs and we can have Carri's old cot when the baby comes. We have to buy a cooker and a second hand three piece suite, but Mam even helps out with that. I don't know what we'd do without her.

So we have our house. It's the first step and I know I'll get that farm one day.

'You and your bloody pigs,' Cath says whenever I mention it, but I know she'll be proud when I get it and with a farm it's only natural to have a few more kids to fill the place, even though Cath keeps saying 'never again.' I don't ask whether she means no more babies or no more, well, no more of that.

Cath gets real big with the baby. The doctor keeps saying the sickness will stop soon, but Cath's really poorly and I do feel for her. She misses the hotel, Chef Cen and the other waitresses, but her sister's just round the corner with her husband, who I never really take to, and their baby, Gethin. I'm not that keen on Nest, she laughs too loud for a woman and swears like a miner, but it's company for Cath and Nest helps out when Cath's legs get really bloated and she can hardly stand up to do the housework. Some days Nest has bruises on her cheek or arm and stays over on the sofa, but she always goes back. She says she knows a leopard never changes its spots, but she keeps going back anyway, so what can anyone do?

I'm not in the room for the birth, of course, but I know it's bad. Afterwards Cath can't stop crying and she hates it when the nurses bring the baby and make her feed the baby herself. She says it's disgusting, feeding a baby like that and I can see how it must be embarrassing.

'Never mind, Cariad,' I tell Cath, 'I'll buy some bottles for when the baby comes home and get the best formula. It won't be for long, Cariad.'

She cheers up for a minute. 'Cow 'n Gate,' she says. 'Don't get that cheap muck Nest fed to Gethin.'

Of course I won't get cheap muck; it has to be the best for my baby girl. We try to talk about the name while Cath is in hospital, but she has some funny ideas. Sharon or Tracey she says, something modern. The names sound clipped and ugly to me. I want something with a bit of class; a proper Welsh name too.

'How about Sarah like my mam?' I say, but Cath just starts crying. Then it comes to me. 'Megan,' I say, pleased with myself. 'Can't get better than that – good enough for your Nain and pretty an' all, just like my baby girl.'

Cath pulls a face, but she loved her Nain so I know she'll agree. Mam says she likes Megan and I should register the baby straight away, so I do, while Cath's in hospital. She cries over the birth certificate when I show her, but the nurse says it's the way girls are when they've just had a baby and not to worry.

I have to wait ten days for them to come home. I can't believe how long ten days can feel, but there they are at last, my wife and my daughter, Catherine Mary and Megan Sarah, with my mam round to help out most days so there's always a dinner waiting for me. We'll have a son next, I think, but I wouldn't wish Megan to be anything different and it'll be nice for the boy to have a big sister, like I had. Menna always looked out for me when I was a kid.

I don't think life can get more perfect. It's hard of course. Cath doesn't settle down and stop crying, like the nurse said she would, and she doesn't like to touch the baby much, but she's tired and it was such a hard birth, something to do with stirrups and being cut so I know to stay away for a good while.

Megan cries a lot. Cath's the oldest of her family and I thought she'd be a dab hand with babies, but even Cath says she's never heard a baby cry so much. Megan curls up in a ball and screams. She goes so red it scares me sometimes. I have an idea it's something to do with the milk, my mam says it's too heavy for her little stomach and full of sugar, but Cath won't think about feeding Megan herself, so that's that.

It seems to help the baby if I hold her. I put her on my shoulder, rub her back and walk with her; we must have walked miles round that house, me and Megan. It feels like it goes on forever, that time when all she does is cry and I have to pace around with her, but it's not that long really, they soon grow up.

Megan is the spit of Cath, real pretty and clever. I know dads are bound to say it, but it's true – she's not just bright, she's special. She knows every nursery rhyme in the book at two and starts to read when she's three. I don't know where she gets it from and Cath says she doesn't either. Cath looks uncomfortable when she says it.

Megan is three and I haven't so much as laid a finger on Cath since she was first expecting her. It isn't easy, but what can I do? Cath doesn't cry anymore, but she's always angry. It's like every little thing is sent to irritate her. I still think about the farm, but it seems far off now. It's hard with only my wage coming in; sometimes we run out of sugar for our tea and there's no more till the next pay day. We get by, somehow. You get used to how things are, but I get fed up sometimes with Cath's moods and the shouting. Still, I try not to react too much for the sake of the kid. I bite my tongue more times than I can count, but sometimes Cath gets to ranting and I can see it's scaring Megan so I have to say something and Cath doesn't take kindly to being spoken to.

I can calm her down if I'm really careful, but she won't give in to me no matter what I say. She says it's disgusting with Megan asleep in her cot next to us and I suppose she's got a point, so I have to manage without and I wonder if I'll ever get my son. One day when my mam has taken Megan to the park, I try to put my arms round Cath, but she slaps me away as usual.

'Keep your filthy hands to yourself.'

'Come on, Cariad, we could nip upstairs.'

'I've got your dinner in the oven stewing. I can't stand waste.'

'It'll keep, just this once.' We're standing by the fireplace, the coals toasting one side of us, the suck of the air hissing down the chimney. I reach out to her and she picks up the coal shovel and lands me one, catches me right on the funny bone so I feel dizzy and have to sit down on the settee quickly.

'Bloody hell, Cath. There's no need for that!' I rub at my arm and feel my cheeks burning with the rush of the pain and something else. What kind of man gets hit by a woman?

'I told you to keep your filthy hands to yourself and I meant it. I'll get your dinner for you.'

I move to the table and sit in silence. We don't talk while I eat: egg and beans and mash. She sits at the table with me, smoking, not saying a word and I can feel my bile rising, but I just eat. When I'm finished I push the plate away and go through the kitchen out into the yard where the toilet and coal shed are. I smash my fist into the gates between the yard and the back lane till it hurts. When I go back in Cath is washing pots at the sink, her back hunched against me. I slump onto the sofa and wait for Mam to bring Megan home: my warm, soft Megan.

Something in me can't rest after that. I think all the time about having a son, about Cath saying yes for a change. She doesn't, but it happens anyway; it has to happen sooner or later.

Megan likes it at my mam's. She likes playing with Carri and likes all Mam's old clothes and some of Menna's old stuff that she can dress up in. So there's no Megan sleeping lightly in her cot, no-one to disturb, no-one to use as an excuse for not doing anything disgusting. I try to talk Cath into it, but she's having none of that and then somehow I grab her and she starts to cry.

'What? I didn't hurt you.'

'Filthy pig! Men are all the same. Filthy bastards the lot of you.'

Her nail catches on my skin as her hand flails at my face. I can feel the welt across my cheek, sore and angry. I catch both her arms and pin her down. I think I mean to stop her hitting me again, but it's been years, actually years. She cries all the time, turns away and keeps crying when it's all over. I slide out of the bed and go downstairs. I think I'll make some tea, maybe take her a cup, but instead I sit on the sofa, freezing to death in my vest and pants and socks; sit there all night with my head in my hands.

It's not something we can talk about; what could we say? We get on with things, the way we always do. I don't try to touch her again, but she falls anyway and I know I'll get my son. He'll be Edwin James Vaughan like me, this time not Jim, but Edwin.

If anything, the second time round it's even worse for Cath. She throws up all the time and has these headaches that make her moan and wail like she's going to die. I know she hates looking after Megan and Mam helps out a lot, but I have to go to work. Cath cries all the time and when she's not crying, she's shouting, screaming till she changes colour, a horrible blue-white. The more she shouts, the quieter I get. Me and Megan whisper to each other, which makes Cath think we're talking behind her back. One day I come home to find a pan of food kicked all round the house. Megan's Sally-doll is broken on the living room floor and Megan is hiding under the table. The next day I have to get the doctor out and Cath has to go to hospital. Toxaemia, the doctor says.

Cath is there for the last six weeks and the hospital doesn't allow children to visit, but Megan doesn't seem to mind. She goes to my mam's a lot and Gwen down the street has her sometimes when I'm on late shifts. 'She's still wide awake,' Gwen says when I pick Megan up at nearly eleven o'clock. 'My Dafydd's been out for the count for hours, but she never tires does she?'

I smile back. 'Thanks for having her, Gwen. She's never needed a lot of sleep, but I always say she can't be learning anything while she's sleeping,'

When I bring her home I make her a bacon butty with a glass of milk. We watch a late film together and she falls asleep on the rug in front of the fire, always well past midnight.

I like those weeks, just the two of us. Even when she gets chicken pox, she's good as gold. She doesn't scratch them, just lays on the sofa watching telly or doing drawings. She draws me a farm and says we'll live there one day. The one thing I can't do is Megan's hair. It's so fine and long, but it curls too, wild like Cath's before she cut it all off. It's so matted one day that I decide I'll have to have it cut. Properly mind. I take her to a proper women's hairdresser and hover over her like it was an operation and not a haircut. The curls bob round her face when the girl is finished cutting – she looks like one of those church cherubs, only thinner. The girl shows Megan in the mirror.

'There you are, Cariad. Aren't you a picture?'

'No,' Megan says.

'I'll bet your tada likes it,' the girl coaxes.

'Tell him I hate it and I'm not speaking to him.'

She's as good as her word. For a whole week I don't get a word out of her. She tells my mam across the dinner table to give me messages and Mam laughs and passes on the message, but it breaks my heart, the thought of Megan cutting me out like Cath does after one of her rages. I buy Megan a watch, with Snow White on the face and a little soft pink strap. 'Tell him it's very nice,' Megan says to my mother and I want to cry.

It's Carri who does the trick. One morning she gets Megan up, puts her in a lovely new frock that Mam's bought and takes her out onto the flat roof over the side of the shop to have pictures taken. By the time Carri finishes posing her like a model and telling her how lovely her hair is over and over again Megan is her old self.

'I don't want you to ever cut my hair again, though, Tada,' she warns that night over a dinner of fried eggs and mash.

'I won't,' I say, and I mean it.

She looks at her Snow White watch. 'Time for Magpie.' She grins up at me and I feel all my worries melt. 'Are there any good films on later?' It's hard to believe she's only five years old.

I don't get a son after all. We call the new baby Elin, Elin Angharad: Elin for Cath's mam and Angharad for my Nain. Mam suggests it, she says it's only right, but we should shorten Cath's mam's first name — Elin instead of Elinor. I know I won't ever have a son and that the train set I bought is going to stay in its box forever.

Elin is a quiet baby. I think Cath rubs brandy on her gums to keep her sleepy, but I'm not going to say anything. Best to keep the peace. Cath wants an indoor bathroom now that we've got two kids, but I don't know where the money's coming from to pay for another move.

Then her brothers show up, first one, then another. I don't mind so much and it means we can't start to save a bit of money. They have a rough life with Cath's dad. Patrick's coming up to twenty-one and been to sea, but he hates it and gets a job at the Oakley mine as a cook in the canteen. He doesn't want to risk it back home, big as he is, so he comes to us instead. The back bedroom's always been empty, so it's no bother and he's good with Megan, plays with her like he's a kid himself, but I have to watch the drinking, he gets drunk too often for my liking and I won't have that near Megan.

Tom arrives a year later, he's fifteen and he's started to fight with his dad. 'About bloody time,' Cath says, which seems a·bit odd, but, fair play to Tom, he's a good kid and it's not a very happy family. Tom's funny and Megan loves him. So there we are, the two of them in one double bed in the spare room, the four of us in our room and we have some money coming in so we'll be able to get somewhere with an indoor bathroom.

Cath wants to go back to Criccieth, where we had those nice little rooms near the sea and maybe she'll try for a job back in a hotel once Elin is a bit bigger. She's never really settled in Blaenau and the sea air would do Megan good, but it would be a long way to work every day. What I'd like is a bit of garden. In the end my mam sorts things out. She gives us a deposit to buy a bigger place. It's still in Blaenau, but well off the high street with three bedrooms and a bit of garden. There are hardly any cars up and down the road.

She has a nasty cough, my mam, and looks a bit drawn, but we don't think about it being something bad. I think she knew herself though. When the doctor says she has to go in for an operation she goes for the knife drawer and says she may as well end it now. My dad has to stop her, but afterwards I can't get those words out of my head: 'Once they open me up I won't be coming home.'

She's supposed to move to the convalescence home on the day she finally goes. We're all there, Dad, Hugh, Menna, me and Alun; not Carri – it's too much for Carri, she shouldn't be motherless at seventeen, it isn't right. The world isn't right.

'I don't understand it,' I say to Hugh, 'They were moving her today. How could they have thought of moving her to convalescence when she's this bad?'

Hugh rolls his eyes and looks over at Menna. 'For pity's sake, Jim!' He says and storms out of the room.

'She was never going to convalesce, Jim,' Menna says, almost in a whisper. 'They just couldn't do anything else for her.'

Mam always said I was soft in the head and I feel it now, a real pen dafad. I can't believe she's gone, I can't accept it; it's too much to bear and it seems wrong that I can go on breathing while she's lying there, lifeless.

No-one can comfort me, not for ages. I wander around at night, crying or sitting on the stairs like I'm a ghost myself. Cath takes Elin into our bedroom at night, saying Elin has bad dreams. But I've never noticed them. I'm shut out now. Cath and Elin sleep in the double bed, and when I'm finally exhausted enough to sleep, shattered from walking the landing and stairs blubbing to myself, I crawl into the narrow bed in the back bedroom that used to be Elin's. Sometimes it's so lonely in there. Everyone has to have some comfort. We all need a bit of human warmth. Cath won't let me in and Megan is there, with her own little room, soft and warm. But that's not something I like to dwell on.

The first time I see Cath, it's autumn and Jimmy Stewart is making great movies. I've never seen hair that colour and I think: I'm going to marry that girl. It seems so simple – a lovely wife, sons and daughters, a farm with pigs.

Lunch

Megan enters the room before Cath. Her father is hunched deep into the chair, eyes closed, far away. Megan sighs and Jim opens his eyes.

'You need bloody sleep,' Cath hisses arms folded across the landslide of her breasts. 'Don't suppose you get much sleep at night with a conscience as black as yours.'

Megan thinks of mentioning that 'bad' and 'black' are not the same thing, but she is too weary.

'Could do with another cup of tea, Cariad. Actually, I'm a bit famished.'

Megan thinks of the food in the cupboards: pasta and salads, hardly food she can offer Jim and Cath. 'How about a walk? There's a café down at the mall, lots of stalls so you can choose what you want, and we could get a bit of sun on the way; it's such a lovely day.'

'Stalls?' Cath asks suspiciously.

'Little booths. All around a big seating area; there's Chinese and...'

'Don't want no foreign muck,' Cath interjects.

'Well, baked potatoes then,' Megan says biting back what she'd prefer to say, 'or sandwiches or fish and chips. There's all sorts.'

'That sounds alright,' Jim sounds like he is trying to coax a wild animal, Megan thinks. 'I wouldn't mind stretching my legs.'

'Fish 'n chips'll do as long as there's no blacks serving. I don't want their filthy hands on...'

'That's enough, Mam.'

'Don't you tell me...'

'Let's just have a nice walk, eh?'

Jim's voice is the voice of the dad she had when she was five. She flashes him a smile.

'I'm sure there'll be something you like, Mam and it's a lovely walk. They've re-flooded one of the timber docks and put parkland all round it; it's a lovely walk.'

'It's not too far, is it? I can't be doing with walking too far at my age.'

Megan allows herself to laugh. 'You're fifty-two, Mam, not a hundred. You can manage a ten minute walk.'

'Feel like a hundred after what that swine's put me through.'

Jim and Megan say nothing.

It's quiet in the park and the July air thrums with heat. Megan tries to walk ahead to give her parents the chance to walk together, but instead Jim catches her up. Megan slows their pace, but Cath walks behind, huffing a little, her green eyes rimmed red.

In the mall Cath refuses to stand on the escalator to travel to Sunny Quays' restaurant balcony so they walk the length of the mall to find the broad spiral of stairs. Jim surveys the café with interest. 'Not bad this, eh?'

'Bit bloody confusing, isn't it? How're you supposed to decide?'

'Just take your time, Mam, there's no hurry.'

'Fancy a bit o' pie and mash, Love?' Jim nods over to the booth proclaiming 'Traditional Fare' in curly green script on a biscuit-coloured banner. Cath follows Jim's gaze, wrinkles her nose at the girl behind the counter: dreadlocks held back in a striped silk band.

'Not much traditional about that.'

'They have to wash their hands, Cath, they have all this health and safety these days.'

'How do I know she didn't touch it when it was being made?'

'Because it's all brought in, Mam — places like this don't cook from scratch, but then again at the factory, they might not have applied your stringent selection criteria on their staff, so you can't really be sure about anything you eat and you certainly shouldn't go drinking tea the way you do. Don't you realise hardly any white people pick it?'

Megan stalks towards the Thai noodle bar.

'She's always been moody,' Cath confides to Jim. 'I suppose I'll have pie then and a pot of tea,' she adds defiantly.

The restaurant is crowded, even though it is only a few minutes past twelve. Jim hovers with Cath in the over-lit balcony area, trying to adjust to his surroundings. He scans the other customers and wonders what it is that unnerves him about them; there is something not quite right. They are not the pasty, familiar people he left behind but an assortment of shapes and colours. He watches a woman with pale, feathery hair release a chubby toddler from a pushchair. The toddler is dark-skinned with a frizz of wiry, black hair. Mixed race, Jim notes with a shock of recognition, colouring in case Cath is reading his thoughts. To distract himself he glances at two girls, bone thin, their school uniforms worn for maximum leg exposure, their white blouses unbuttoned to show the lace edging on flimsy bras.

'Don't mind me,' Cath cuts into Jim's thoughts.

'Pardon?'

'I'll give you pardon. I'm not daft you know, ogling kids now. Is that how old your fancy bit was?'

'I'll get the pies.'

When Jim returns Cath is glaring angrily around. 'Took you long enough, where's Megan?'

'Seems very popular, this place. I think she was chatting to a friend she bumped into.'

'Very nice,' Cath snorts.

They begin to eat. The gravy is a little congealed and the vegetables are watery, but Jim takes comfort in the familiarity of hearty mediocre food.

'I could have had anyone you know,' Cath blurts suddenly over a forkful of soggy carrots.

'I'm sure you could. You eat up, Love.'

'Don't try to shut me up. I had prospects. A French boy wanted to marry me, you know. He took me dancing and everything; he was heart-broken when they sent him home.'

Jim nods. He pushes a piece of pie crust around his plate, struggles to think of something to say.

'You needn't think I missed you, you know.'

'Right.'

'I missed having someone to drive me, but I stay with Elin most of the time, so she drives. She's a very good driver, Elin, not fast, like you. I have to tell her sometimes "Put your foot down, Elin, get a move on". And then there was the money. I'd never even signed a cheque before. All these women burning their bras years ago and I don't even know how to change a plug. It's the small things that you notice.'

Like a smile, Jim thinks. Like Consuela propped on one elbow smiling at him as he wakes up every morning. A surge of loneliness slaps him as he looks at Cath's face. He reaches a hand towards the dry, red skin of Cath's hands.

'I'm taking you back because that's how things are.' She moves her hand away as though he is an insect.

'You're what I married and I don't see why I should be on my own at my age.'

'At my age, Jim, I want someone real,' Consuela had said.

'You get to an age where you realise the choices were made a long time ago,' Jim says, wondering if he should have spoken aloud.

'What?'

'I mean, at our age, you realise where you belong.'

'Some of us never forgot,' Cath spits back.

Had she always known that he would come back? Was it all 'meant' like his mam always said?

They have almost finished the plates of pie, mash and vegetables when Megan arrives back at the table.

'Sorry, ran in to a friend, Jo. I thought it would give you bit of time to chat.' She sits down to finish the remains of her noodles.

Cath surveys the mixture of faces around them. 'Country's going to the dogs.'

Megan glances at her Mother; Cath's face has the soggy look of someone about to cry, though she is more likely to break into vitriol. 'Would you like anything else to drink?' Megan asks, too cheerfully.

'No.'

'I'm fine as I am, Cariad,' Jim says. 'Not a bad cup of tea that.'

'Okay, we'll take a slow stroll home, then, shall we?' Megan is aware of trying too hard. She wants to be able to go home and sleep. She has an urge to play her pregnancy card, to claim the need for an afternoon rest and kid glove treatment, but she suspects it will only enrage Cath.

'Unless you want another drink, Cariad,' Jim adds, nodding towards Megan. 'Probably have to keep your fluids up with...you know—for the baby.'

'She's fine. It's only a bloody baby and she's not very far along. Don't even know if it'll take yet. She might lose it.'

'I'm fifteen weeks, Mam.'

'Still, can't count your chickens. Bit old for a first baby, anyway. Hope there won't be anything wrong with it.'

'I'm twenty-nine, Mam, not forty.'

'Whatever you say; you always know best. Never did listen to me. You wouldn't believe I'd brought up two kids myself, the way I'm ignored.'

Megan closes her eyes. 'I'm fine, Dad. We can get another drink when we get home.'

'It might be a boy,' Jim says, but his eyes look far away.

They lapse back into silence on the walk home. The sky has clouded and there is a cooler feel in the air.

Downhill

Walking back to Megan's house, Cath tries to remember the first film that Jim took her to see — something with Jimmy Stewart in it, no doubt.

She would rather be dancing, even on this first date; people think dancing is a bit risqué, but it's safer than sitting down in a gloomy cinema where a hand can creep around you before you've noticed it. Jim is respectful, though, not pushy, like some boys. He says he loves her red hair, but she watches him looking at her figure when he thinks she isn't taking any notice. Cath is always vigilant. She likes his name, Edwin James Vaughan, a family name and he lets her take her time telling him where she lives, doesn't seem put out to be dating a girl from Holyhead, not that he should be put out, but there are some boys who put on airs or get the wrong impression. She likes his mam too, wishes Elinor could be like Sarah, hard working and blunt, but kind. She'll do anything for Jim, anything for the girl that marries Jim, Cath thinks.

She likes to tell people she's married: Mrs Vaughan. Even more she likes to tell them about the flat in Criccieth. The two rooms sparkle and Cath lets in the sea air every day to keep the place fresh. She's a silver service waitress at a real hotel and Jim works hard. Cath skips to work, she is nineteen and happy. One day she'll have her own house by the sea. Jim wants a farm and lots of brats running around making a mess, but he'll forget about that. It's the other thing that worries her, if only he would forget about that. She's a married woman, it's not like she can say no every time, but without it life would be perfect. Most nights she slaps Jim away, rolls out of reach of his sloppy kisses. Like a dog, she thinks with distaste. But some nights he gets his way, despite the brushed cotton nightdress that she refuses to take off.

Cath hates the thought of the baby, hates moving to Blaenau, though at least it's a house; a start, she reassures herself. Evans is handy for shopping and Jim's Mam helps out a lot, but the baby threatens to overwhelm her, bloating her so that her legs ache constantly and her back is a mass of pain.

The delivery suite is white, so white it hurts. The pain in Cath's back feels like a mess of bruised organs leaking blood and bile into her abdomen. She feels as though someone has kicked her repeatedly. It is unbelievable to feel such pain and still be alive. She hates Jim, she hates the baby.

She will never go through this again, this pain and humiliation. The nurse shouts instructions at Cath so that her head rings with them, but still she can't make sense of what she's told. She hears her name over and over.

'Mrs Vaughan... Mrs Vaughan...' but she can't catch the other barked words through the thick fog of pain. She feels her legs lifted and hears her own cries, far off and chilling, as the stirrups are fitted. The screaming hurts her ears.

'That's enough of that, Mrs Vaughan, you're not helping yourself.'

Cath sobs, sinks back, her legs splayed in the unthinkable stirrups, everything on view. She closes her eyes as the nurse picks up metal implements to hand to the doctor, who is gazing inside her and slowly shaking his head. She opens one eye to feel for the mask and breathes in the gas. As the cutting begins, Cath sobs and inhales. 'Trilene', the nurse called it. 'Trilene', she says the word to herself over and over like a useless prayer as pain and nausea compete.

Afterwards the nurses on the ward tut over Cath's distaste at feeding the baby.

'Now come along, Mrs Vaughan, we can't have any of this silliness. You're a mam now.'

The flabby sister with big rough red hands pulls on Cath's nightdress and she begins to cry.

'None of that now.' The sister jiggles the baby in her arms. 'This baby needs its milk.'

'I don't want...' Cath begins, her voice thin and tearful.

'Well the time for thinking about that was when you got in the family way. You've had your fun and now it's time to pay up, I'm afraid.'

Cath hunches down in the raised metal hospital bed and bites her lip while the sister looms over her, continues to bully her into exposing her breast. Cath manages to insist on the curtains being pulled round the bed while the baby chews on her nipple, ineffectual except for causing more pain. Cath can feel her breasts swelling, becoming rock hard like cartoon breasts that might explode at any moment. They don't explode, they only become harder, more inflamed, more painful. There is pain everywhere: the granite breasts, the places inside her where the cuts rub against the stitches, her abdomen, her back.

After the hospital she is alone with it. It — Megan, a name that sounds like putty. She didn't choose this baby, the birth, the name, any of it. She wants to curl up and forget, but the baby screams, constantly, violently, until she wants to shake it silent. She leaves the baby screaming in its pram for fear of what she will do if she touches it. Cath sits on the sofa by the unmade fire in her faded candlewick dressing gown, buries her head in her hands, sobs and rocks until she and the baby both wear themselves out with the tears.

When she wakes she is always cold, always parched dry and hungry. The baby is always screaming. She tries to feed the baby. The bottles are sterilised, clean. No-one can accuse of her being dirty like her mam, but the baby spews back most of what Cath manages to dribble into her. Sometimes the baby vomits whole streams of foul-smelling milk across the room before it pulls up its thin legs, balls itself tight, screws up a reddening face and bawls to wake the dead.

It goes on forever: the exhaustion, the crying, not knowing where the baby's misery stops and her own begins. At some point the thing becomes a toddler, a precocious thing with thin red curls and her own eyes looking back at her. But they are different eyes, more knowing. Cath imagines the child watching her all the time, taking her in like some specimen. Everyone marvels at Megan, the way she can speak, the way she will sit for hours watching the adults. It unnerves Cath. She wonders if she has spawned something strange and alien. She even asks Sarah if she thinks Megan is normal, if she's alright: perhaps the forceps at the birth have done some damage; perhaps she is not like other children. But Sarah only laughs.

Cath won't let it happen again. At night she warns Jim to keep his hands to himself, she whispers that he will wake Megan, that he'll frighten the child to death. That keeps him off her. She frightens herself one day, the day that Jim tries something in the living room and she hits him with the shovel. But when the fear subsides she knows he won't hit back, that she has the upper hand now and a huge surge of relief sweeps through her.

The next time she hits him it's in self defence, but he doesn't stop. He forces her like some alley cat caught by the bins. She cries herself to sleep afterwards. She cries all the time now, like she did after Megan was born: unannounced tears welling up at unpredictable times and places to shame her. She cries and she throws up: thin mucous streams of bile in the mornings, whole meals later in the day or whenever some smell takes her guts by surprise. She knows she is pregnant again and wants to rip the thing out. Every day is worse than the last one until the day when she finally kicks the pan all around the house. It is a long time since she felt so light-headed, so elated, but it doesn't last. She feels worn out and defeated by the time Jim arrives home and takes Megan's side as usual.

Her blood pressure shoots up the next day and she has to be admitted to hospital; to peace and quiet with park views and no children allowed — the best six weeks of her life if only she could forget the thing growing inside her.

Through the blood and pain Cath can hear snatches of urgent shouting, very far away, she thinks. Someone says something about a breach, about a baby doubled up, someone says something in hushed tones — *it can't possibly live, we're going to lose the mother.* Between the whispers, far away people shout at her: push, stop, breath, push, more. She wants to shout back, but her

96

voice doesn't work, the words are lost, suffocated by the insistent wailing scream that is coming from her.

Jim tells Cath they'll call the baby Elin. Sarah's idea. Elin for her mam, Elinor. The radio is playing somewhere off the ward and Cath can hear a song playing. *Second-hand Rose.* Cath likes the tune, it's catchy. Rose is a nice short name and it must be modern with the song playing it all the time, but Sarah and Jim are fixed on Elin. Let them name her, but this baby will be hers. This baby won't scream all the time, she'll sleep, the brandy will see to that. Good as gold, everyone will say.

Cath has an ordinary docile baby, and she has her brothers living with her. She feels safer with the boys sleeping in the next door room. It won't happen again.

When Sarah dies Cath weeps real tears, but she can't compete with Jim. She wonders if he will cry for her like that when the time comes, but she knows the answer. She misses Sarah. And Jim's dad won't be as generous without Sarah to cajole him. But there has to be a limit to grief. Jim should get on with living now. When Jim keeps crying, haunting the place with his dry sobs, she takes Elin into her room. Jim's out of her bed for good now. He can sleep in the back room.

She would like to go back to being a silver service waitress, but she's not nineteen with a good figure anymore and Elin is a clingy child, not independent like Megan. Cath doesn't know who she might leave Elin with: not with her mother or with Nest, who is pregnant for the fourth time and who leaves and goes back to Tony faster than Cath can blink. Anita offers to lend a hand, but she's two buses away and, at twenty-one, Anita has her own two babies to look after and a husband that Cath wouldn't leave a dog with. She will have to wait until Elin goes to school before she can find a job, then she will try to find something local that fits in with the short school day. Maybe she could get a part time job just waitressing lunches, she tells herself, trying not to think that she will be a saggy thirty-three year old by then.

The mortgage payments are a struggle without the extra help from Sarah, even though Jim works all the overtime he can get, and Jim's nocturnal wanderings bother her, but she shuts him out and tries to do something about Elin being so clingy — she can't even go to the toilet alone and sometimes has an urge to kick Elin away.

She feels herself becoming more shapeless and voluminous, like some out of control jelly. She avoids looking at her body, but wishes that she had looked at it at more when it was shapely. She wills herself to remember, but can't conjure it, even in imagination. She avoids the bath, splashing herself perfunctorily in the bathroom sink, avoiding eye contact with the mirror as she does so. She calls it a strip wash, but there is never any stripping as she slides herself carefully from day to night clothes, clothes as loose-fitting and formless as one another. Cath catches a smell sometimes, a yeasty, fleshy smell that makes her scrub the kitchen and bathroom in a frenzy, but it never helps.

When Elin finally goes to school Cath succumbs to nightmares. There is something terrible about the pitiable way that Elin has to be prised away from her, dragged screaming into the classroom each day by an increasingly unsympathetic teacher. Elin reminds Cath of Patrick, the way he would cling to door handles or tables as he was dragged off for a thrashing. At night she lies awake for hours, resisting the images of sleep that will eventually overtake her. Patrick's screams and the heft of the belt cutting the air with its thwacking sound slide into images of school. She is eleven years old, her hand held palm down on the desk for the bite of a ruler or palm up for the cane while she stands in front of the whole class, her humiliation on display.

In her nightmares the bedroom door creaks and she is dragged, sleep-sodden, into the bathroom by her dad at two in the morning, pushed up against the wall and told to keep quiet. She half wakes to another squeak, but it is only the sound of Megan's bedroom door. Cath buries her head into the pillow. She has to sleep in the daytime to make up for the exhaustion. It only takes a tot of brandy to secure a few hours of dreamless sleep. The headaches start gradually, black storms that gather around her head and implode there, angry and raucous.

'How's Mam today?' Cath hears Megan asking Jim.

'She's got one of her headaches, Cariad.'

'Shall I boil her an egg?'

'That would be nice. Maybe you could do a couple for you and Elin? For tea? I'll cut soldiers for you.'

Cath imagines the scene: Megan smiling at Jim with that knowing smile of hers, more like an indulgent elderly aunt than an eleven-year-old.

The doctor pronounces migraines, very severe he says, and bad nerves – both conditions which cannot tolerate noise. Megan sits in her bedroom, reading library books – the classics, Cath boasts to neighbours when she isn't sick. But Elin is harder to keep quiet. One day Elin takes one of Jim's heavy spanners to her dolls, pounding their heads to plastic splinters. She kicks a ball at the living room window. An accident, she says when interrogated. She screams loudly when Jim tries to wash her hair in the bath on Sunday afternoon, so that Cath is forced to hobble out of bed, scowling, her head cupped in her hands, eyes screwed tight against the light.

'I should have put my head in a gas oven while I had the chance.'

'You go back to bed, Love. I'll see to this.'

'Sounds like it.'

'She's just a kid. You go and lie down. I'll get Megan to put the kettle on.'

Cath hears the front door and freezes in bed. Footsteps creep up the stairs one at a time, pausing on every step. Megan. But it's only two in the afternoon. Cath listens to Megan tiptoe across the landing, then slide open her bedroom door.

'Who's there?' Cath's voice is heavy and slurred.

She pictures Megan's face, all condescension. 'It's only me, Mam.'

'What you think you're bloody up to at this time of day? Trying to make me bad? Frightening the life out of me? Why aren't you at school?'

Megan appears at her bedroom door and peers into the gloom. Cath wonders if Megan notices the smell: sour and stale, but Megan won't recognise this.

'What you crinkling your nose up at, Lady Muck?'

'Nothing – just a...'

'Just a what?'

'A funny smell, like that pub when Sian got married.'

Cath pictures the dingy bar where her younger sister had her wedding reception last month. Seventeen years old and already eight months gone.

'You mind your manners, Megan Vaughan. I'll give you "funny smell".' Cath breathes in her room: old sweat and old alcohol, cigarette smoke graining the air. Of course Megan would notice. 'What are you doing home, anyway?'

'I had a nosebleed,' Megan whispers.

'You and your bloody nosebleeds! Don't go letting your stupid father see any blood. You know what he's like with blood. Bloody fool.'

Megan nods and fixes her green eyes on the thin smear of egg trailing down the front of Cath's brushed cotton nightdress where her old candlewick dressing gown, threadbare now, is open at the front.

'What do you think you're gawping at?'

'Nothing.'

'Go and make me a cup of tea and don't go bloody bleeding into it.'

'Okay, Mam.'

'Okay, Mam,' Cath apes. She moves in bed and something hits the carpet with a thud, rolls softly and tinkles to a standstill by the bedside cabinet.

Megan moves forward to pick up the bottle.

'You leave that alone!'

'Okay, Mam.'

'I'm going to the bathroom.' Cath sways slightly as she gets to her feet, steadies herself against the bedside cabinet as she reaches down for the almost empty bottle, tucks it under the bed-covers and walks towards the bathroom, her steps tentative and shaky.

Cath knows that Megan is listening as she retches and vomits. She turns to shout downstairs, but the world spins.

When Cath opens her eyes Megan is crouched over her. Cath winces at the sight of the sick splashed around the toilet seat. She can feel a drizzle of mucous leaking from her mouth. She watches Megan recoil at the foul smell of her breath: cigarettes, alcohol and vomit. She watches the blood begin to blob from Megan's nose as she stands up.

'I'll fetch Mrs Pritchard,' Megan says, holding onto her nose to staunch the blood.

Cath thinks she will protest, but she is too exhausted.

When Cath comes home from hospital she spends less time in bed. There are fewer headaches, but Cath trails her rage after her like a cloud. She feels as though she is watching herself from a distance, unable to do anything to stop the anger. Dishes fly across the kitchen. The ornaments are depleted, the pottery ones first. Splinters of glass or plaster lurk in the carpets to pierce unwary feet. On her darkest days Cath throws knives from the kitchen drawers, not aimed, but scattered ominously. Sometimes she tips the contents of her bedroom drawers over the banisters. One day she hurls the whole drawer down after the clothes.

When she has finished the destruction she sits on the bottom stair, rocking and weeping and wishing she could be someone else.

'Your Nanna Vaughan gave me those drawers,' Cath sobs when Megan shuffles towards her anxiously. Megan pats her, fetches a tea towel for her to dry her eyes and begins gathering up the mess of clothes.

When Megan is finished, Cath allows herself to be shepherded to bed. She lies awake, listening to the sounds of the house, to Megan patiently explaining that Mam isn't well, that Jim must fix the drawers. Cath listens to Elin whimpering as Megan tucks her in bed, into Megan's single bed.

'Shush, Elin, there's a good girl, you can sleep with me while Mam is poorly.'

'Jim sleeps in the spare room,' Cath whispers aloud as she falls asleep.

Jim balks at the idea of going abroad, but there are no jobs at home and Cath is decided on it. They have to have some money coming in. Jim tries window-cleaning after he is made redundant, but he's too slow and conscientious to make a living at it and Cath is enraged by the pitiful takings he brings home. A cousin of his, a plumber, puts a few odd jobs his way, but it's not enough to keep a family.

Cath leaves adverts around at first: big spreads in the newspapers about jobs in Saudi, Kuwait or Algeria. She lets the adverts seep in before she starts making suggestions. A steady stream of families is leaching from Blaenau, but Cath can't face moving. She feels relief when Jim signs up to work for an American company running a desalination plant in Algeria. Megan is fifteen now. The spare bed looks as though it has been slept in these days, but Cath can't take chances; it's better that Jim works away.

Jim paints Megan's bedroom yellow before he leaves. She has the biggest bedroom in the house now. 'She needs somewhere she can study,' Jim insists, but it niggles at Cath, the way he makes such a fuss of

Megan. She hears Jim telling Megan to "look after everyone" before he leaves.

Cath sits at the kitchen table. It's quiet in the house without Jim. Not that he ever says much, she thinks, but she misses him. It riles her to miss him. She misses how his presence sends her into furies of screaming or throwing, sometimes pounding him with some object that comes to hand. There is none of that without him. She misses the rush of blood in her ears, her heart pounding; the leap of energy before the calm that she only feels after something is hurt or destroyed.

She thinks about Megan, how Jim still goes to Megan for advice, for her opinion. 'I'm his bloody wife,' she hisses to the too-quiet room.

When she goes upstairs she notices Megan's door is open a crack and tiptoes inside. 'I'm his bloody wife,' she says to her sleeping daughter.

It becomes a habit, the way some people might pray at night standing by a bed, a comfort. Jim doesn't keep drink in the house, but he's not there now, and Cath does the shopping with no-one to watch over her shoulder. She has a small glass of gin at night – only one or maybe a couple, she thinks as she totters toward the stairs with uneven steps.

She smiles to think of herself standing by Megan's bed and then it occurs to her. She tiptoes back to the kitchen. Cath grips the kitchen knife that is used for the Sunday roast. In Megan's room she stands by the bed, the light of a passing car suddenly drenching her in grey half-light through the curtains. She raises an arm, watches the blade glint for a second in the receding car light. 'I'm his bloody wife,' she slurs.

After that night Cath never enters Megan's room. She pours away the remaining gin, less than half a bottle, weeping over the sink. She leaves Megan's clean clothes or bedding on the landing outside her door, a new petticoat on top of the pile, real cotton, with lace around the bottom that shows under the peasant skirts young girls wear these days. She won't go into the yellow bedroom again.

Another World

I can't tell them what that place was like, not even Megan. Manila. At least I could say the names. Spanish – some of them sounded like they'd been spat up, but mostly they were easier than the names in Algie.

In Blaenau I think I know what poverty is. Growing up, I see families like Cath's. Holyhead and Blaenau Ffestiniog – not much to choose between them: kids with patched trousers and frocks washed till they hardly have any colour left in them; kids three to a bed or drinking tea out of jam jars. That is all gone, the so-called good old days, but even now there are plenty that go without, even in the family. Patrick can never hold down a job. He gets sober, cleans the house, feeds the kids a good meal, finds work, but a week later it's the same drunken story all over again. I suppose at least he tries. His wife never even gets sober, never cleans up, never lifts a finger for those kids. And then there are Cath's sisters, all married to wasters who knock them around, always on the dole, always on the scrounge. Their kids have nothing. I know what poverty is, but Manila is in a different league.

There are kids here on the street. On the edge of our district – villages, they call them – there's a squatters camp. It's down on the McKinley Rd, where Fort Bonifacio runs out: shacks built too close to the creeks that swarm with mosquitoes and kids. I'll never get used to this. You'd think they'd have some self control, not have so many kids when they can't feed them, but that's Catholics for you. My mam always hated the Catholic Church. I remember her asking Cath about being Catholic. Not that Cath's mam ever went near a church, of course. It wasn't that Mam had anything against the people, Irish or whatever, it was the Church itself. Mam hated how people got told how to live; how they did as they were told. I've never taken much notice before, but in Manila, you can't miss the signs – opiate of the masses, my dad always called it, a quote from some bigwig who wrote about these things, probably some leftist Commie knowing my dad, but out here you can see what he meant.

In Algie we live in the compound. We hear the calls to prayer all the time. We get narked when the Algies keep stopping every five minutes to pray, but when you think about it it's the only bit of their country we notice. We don't go out much: the odd day trip to see the desert, little excursions, but by and large we are shut off from the place. There is no compound in Manila, just the gated villages, full of ex-pats, but not so shut off. The place teems with religion and unwanted children. But I am with Consuela. That's the main thing.

She doesn't expect me to go home with her.

'Tell me about your home, Jim.'

'What about it?'

'What colour is it?'

'Colour? You mean my front door?'

'No, silly.' She has a laugh like rain, not dirty slate and smoke rain, but the sort you get up on the Moelwyns; refreshing.

'The place. What is the colour of the place?' When she puts her head on one side, her black hair falls like one of Cath's velvet curtains.

'I don't think I follow you.'

'In Manila the colour is blue. That's the colour I think of – blue like… like lapis or like…' She searches for the words, sweeping her hair back with both hands lifted. 'The Churches are blue and gold inside. The sea is blue. The sky is blue, pale or blue tinged clouds or that shade between slate and indigo that you get for a moment after dusk, when all the orange and brown of the sun has gone. At home, my home before I went to the city, the mountains on the horizon always looked blue. That is the colour. Places all have a colour, Jim.' She speaks in this one long rush so that I'm dizzy with it; I have to concentrate hard to make out the words.

'Here?'

'White.'

'Hmm.'

'So what colour is your home?'

'Grey.'

'Grey?' That movement of her head again, like she is always puzzling over me.

'Yes, grey. Grey slate and slag heaps everywhere, grey rain, but if you go into the mountains and look down it's an incredible sight. I took...' I trail away.

'Yes?'

'Nothing. It's just grey. My home is grey. Grey slate. Grey houses. Grey sea. Grey sky. Grey rain. Grey people when I come to think about it.'

'What where you going to say, Jim, about the hills, about the lights?'

'Nothing, really.'

'Who did you take? Is it your daughter? Is it Megan?'

She says Megan's name like she's talking through silk. I love that. I shrug and she doesn't press me. I love that too.

'At Christmas I will go back to Manila.'

'Yes. I'll be in Blaenau.'

'And we will not be together, Jim.'

'No, not for two weeks. I'll miss you.'

'No, Jim. I'm going back home. My contract here is finished.'

'What?'

'I'll be staying there, Jim.'

'But...'

The words tumble out, not thought out, not rehearsed in my mind over and over before I let them drop between us: 'I'll come with you.'

I have to do as I've said now. It is set in motion. More than that, it's done.

'To Manila?'

I nod, too choked up to say anything else.

Consuela unfolds herself from the bed where she is sitting, legs tucked up. She crosses the bare, white room, hardly two steps, stands in front of the white wicker chair that creaks under me, holds my face in her hands and releases a long, slow smile.

'We must go outside and see the stars, Jim.' Her hands reach for mine to tug me up like a child at Christmas.

We shiver under the night sky. 'We share the same sky with the people at home, Jim. They are not so far away, just the angles are different, that is all.'

I put an arm round her and we look up, silent and shivering.

Inside, we warm each other, hold on to each other, to the pact we have made and fall asleep still dressed.

I write the note on airmail paper: grey paper, thin paper like the pages of the Bible, the one my mam gave to Megan not long before she died. Grey paper to go to a grey place. I write the note over and over, tearing sheets out of the notepad until there are hardly any left.

I sit with my head in my hands and feel how dry my skin is. I start again. *'Won't be home for Christmas, won't be coming home. Jim.'* It's pathetic, but I fold it into the envelope anyway, address it quickly, before I can change my mind.

We take a taxi from Nikoy Aquino International. The city looks like how I imagine New York, skyscrapers everywhere, traffic jams and noise, but I can see from the trees it's somewhere more foreign. There are crowds everywhere. It's up in the eighties when we arrive, but the temperature's nothing compared to the humidity. I can feel the sweat pooling down my back, the silk sticking to me. We stay in a hotel in Makati city at first, the seedier end, with some rum looking nightclubs nearby.

Consuela has a cousin who is a security guard to a family in an ex-pat village. It's not really a village, just big houses gated off from the natives. The ex-pats bus them in on these official buses so that they can skivvy for them. Jeepneys they call them, painted every colour of the rainbow and churning out filth from their exhausts. It's just like Algie in that way, the Filipinos doing all the dirty work: maids, security guards, cleaners, drivers, pool maintenance, odd jobs, gardening. I suppose that's what they're used to.

This cousin of Consuela's knows someone who works for an estate agent – realtors they call them here, like the Yanks. This friend of the cousin's looks out for a place for us to rent. I bung the cousin a few pesos, some for him, some for his friend, it's all about backhanders here. I have to keep doing the maths in my head to think how much I'm spending, but it seems okay. I've been saving for a good few years now, working abroad. I can keep putting money in the bank for Cath, same as I did when I was in Algie and still live alright here, at least for the time being.

I wonder what the cousin is going to think about Consuela living with me, but he doesn't seem to turn a hair.

'Will your cousin say anything to your family about you living with me?'

'My family know all about you, Jim.'

'They do?'

'Of course, Jim.'

'Not going to get a visit one night from several large brothers and cousins, am I?

Consuela laughs and blushes, but shakes her head.

'Don't they mind? I mean, I thought your family were Catholic?'

Consuela takes a deep breath. 'They don't mind, Jim, but they mind talking about it.'

I must look puzzled. Consuela walks towards me and takes my face in her hands; stands over me looking down fondly.

'In this county many men have...' she pauses, says the word so quietly I can hardly hear her, 'mistresses.'

She takes another deep breath and squats by my chair, head in my lap for a moment, then looks up.

'Many men have another family. It is known, but it is not talked about. If a man's mistress has children and he keeps her seven years then the children are recognised, they can inherit, but it is still never talked of openly. It is very important here...we call it *mukha*...not to lose face.'

'I see,' I say, wondering if I do see. I stroke Consuela's sleek, dark hair; watch the ceiling fan on its winding route creaking round and round. 'How about you show me some sights?'

We are tourists at first, while we are waiting to find a house and living in the not quite nice hotel. We spend a lot of time at the movies. For sixty pesos each the ticket lets us stay there all day. We can bask in the air conditioning, out of the noise and pollution. They have all the big films, only a couple of months behind the Yanks so not much different to home, but the cinema is different. I have to really concentrate, not to get distracted by the people that arrive anytime, wander out in the middle, or bring in whole meals with them. There's always a flag in the corner. The first time we're there I'm a bit surprised when everyone stands to sing the national anthem, all facing the flag.

When we're not at the pictures, we do the things that tourists do: we watch the boats across Manila bay, the little fishing canoes with their outriders to balance them when the nets are thrown, the big container ships anchored further out; we walk on the thin strip of beach that is sheltered by tropical forest trees or take a ride on a Calesas through the Intramuros or Chinatown district, the one they call Binundo. I like the Calesas, the clop of the horses and the streets that look like something out of a postcard of Spain or France with narrow roads, tall buildings with crumbling fronts and little balconies, but it's not real life.

I go with Consuela to the bazaars, full of colour and noise. She buys a thin, beautiful quilt for the bed we will have when we get a house, two embroidered cushions and a door screen of rattling white and pink shells threaded together. There is stall after stall of people selling silverwork in the bazaar: spoons with fancy designs on the handles, intricate jewellery. For

Christmas, I buy Consuela a necklace with a little silver heart, just the edge of the heart around an open space, and, in the space, held there on tiny chain links, a horseshoe for luck. I think of my mother, who always liked the races, always had a horseshoe for luck outside her front door. They believe in luck here and in love.

It doesn't take the cousin long to find us a place to rent, but there's an argument.

'It is a bad house, Pablo, you know this.'

Pablo smiles. They do that, here, smile for yes or no, smile when there is some disaster and smiling is all you can do not to cry.

'But Consuela, you know houses come up for rent in June, nearly all of the houses. It is lucky to find a house in January.'

'It is only available because it is unlucky.'

'Unlucky?' I ask.

'This house had a bad thing.'

'The people in it before were American,' Pablo explains, running a hand through hair that is damp with humidity and frustration. 'They had a baby and something went wrong. They've gone back to America.'

'Did it die?' I ask.

'It just wasn't right, something wrong with it.' He turns back to Consuela with his palms outstretched. 'It's not the house that made it happen, Consuela. It is a good house, good district, three bedrooms and a pool.'

'We don't need three bedrooms and a pool just attracts mosquitoes. You want us to get dengue?'

'Of course I don't want you to get dengue. The pool has pumps and there are no creeks near the house. You have to burn mosquito coils and put down Baygon mats everyday in this hotel, so what's the difference?'

'It has six steps.' Consuela crosses her arms across her body and looks triumphant, eyes flashing with defiance.

Pablo throws his hands in the air and sits on the bed. He curls his head into his arms with an exaggerated groan. 'Mary and all the saints preserve me from this superstitious woman!'

'What's the problem with six steps?' I ask, baffled.

Pablo looks up. 'If a house has steps and the steps are divisible by three it is supposed to be bad luck.' He smiles whenever he talks to me, but I hear the stress on 'supposed' and see Consuela flash him that look of immovability again.

'It is very bad luck,' Consuela adds. She looks like a child about to stamp her foot and cry loudly, a look I've never seen before on her smiling face. 'And the doors are wrong.'

'The doors?'

I get no answer from Pablo, who only groans again and says something under his breath in Filipino, something that draws a sharp look from Consuela.

'The front and back doors are opposite each other, straight through.'

'And that's bad luck too?' I can't help but smile and at least Consuela smiles back. She reaches out to take my hands and looks me in the face. I want to pull her to me, but remember about the *mukha*: private life is private or people lose face.

'Feng shui,' she says simply, and I raise my eyebrows in question.

'Superstition,' Pablo tosses in.

'Not so. It is very well respected. There are geomancers who will align your whole house for you, but with the doors like that the entire chi will just run straight out. It is no good.'

I take my hands from Consuela and rub my brow. I have no idea what chi is, but I'm resigned to never understanding. Some things just are, I think, like not walking under ladders or standing on the cracks in the pavement. My mam always swore by those things.

'Sorry, Pablo, maybe we should wait for another place.'

'You might have a long wait.'

'So it seems, mate, but Consuela knows what she wants. Thanks for your trouble, but I think we'll hang on for now.'

When Pablo leaves I walk outside our hotel door with him, slip him a few more pesos without saying anything, just a smile. I think I'm getting the hang of *mukha*.

When I go back inside Consuela is all smiles. She throws her long arms around my neck, stands on tiptoe to reach my face with her lips. 'You are a very good man, Jim.'

It's April before Pablo and his friend come up with another house. Not such a good district, Pablo says, but he means not such a good district for a European. We could live in one of those crumbling old districts tomorrow for next to nothing, fifty quid a month perhaps, but whites don't live there and Pablo insists we wouldn't be safe.

The house Pablo's friend finds is a little town house, about thirty years old perhaps, two bedrooms and a high concrete wall all around it. It has ten steps, so Pablo says it won't flood and Consuela can't divide them by three. Fort Bonifacio is full of Yanks and they're friendly enough, a bit distant when they realise Consuela's not my maid, but that suits us anyway, we're happy enough with our own company. We don't have our own security guard, but I know Pablo's friends are looking out for us on the quiet, the thing is not to mention it, just to keep giving him a few pesos.

We're not short of a bob or two, but I know the money won't last forever and anyway, I'm not much of a one for sitting around doing nothing. I have a word with Pablo and by June I have a job with an American company that recruits security guards for its staff's housing. They want someone to oversee the guards and they like the idea of having a Brit, someone who won't take bribes they say and won't turn a blind eye when a guard is reported for getting too friendly with the family's maid or is found out for taking some drug they're into called *shubu*.

It's not the kind of thing I've done before, but I make my last job in Algie as a warehouse foreman sound like there was a lot of paperwork and it seems like the job's mostly about summing people up, seeing through the ones who are on the take, the kind you wouldn't want standing near your house with a billy club.

Consuela says she will find a job too, but I don't like the idea of that.

'Jim, in my country, women work.'

'I thought it'd be a bit more traditional here?'

'Women look after the house. Men are what you call breadwinners, but still women usually work too.'

'I don't want you cleaning people's houses.' It sounds peevish out loud, but she smiles.

116

'What if I make quilts? I have a cousin with a stall at the bazaar. You remember the stall where I bought our quilt? Will you like that?'

There is no hint of sarcasm in her voice, she is waiting for me to say yes or no. At that moment I love her totally.

'That sounds okay to me.'

She smiles again. 'Good. I wanted to ask you something else.'

'Yes?'

'It is a holiday soon, for Independence Day.'

'June 12th,' I say, proud of my budding local knowledge.

'I thought we might make a trip to Luzon and you can meet my family.'

I stand up and sit down again. 'Well...'

I stand again and run my hands through my hair. It feels greasy in the heat. The humidity in the air presses closer. I ache for the storm to break. I sit down again.

'They want to meet me?'

'Of course. They are very proud of where I live, that you look after me so well.'

'Ah.'

'You will come to Baguio with me? We have the best strawberries in all the Philippines.' She nestles next to me, edging my arm around her the way a puppy might.

'Strawberries, eh? Megan...'

She sits away from me slightly, takes my face in her hands for just a moment. 'It is alright to say their names, Jim. Maybe not to my family,' she laughs, easing the tension, 'but to me. I know you love your daughters.'

'Strawberries are Megan's favourite.'

'And tomatoes?'

'Tomatoes?'

'Baguio has the best tomatoes too. I go to the market at Greenbelt Park on Saturdays for them.'

'Ah. Megan never liked tomatoes. I used to grow them in my greenhouse, red ones and yellow ones. Cath used to make them into soup, it was one of the few times she cooked, when the tomatoes were ripe. Megan and Elin wouldn't eat them raw.

I used to sell a few on to the local greengrocer, it paid for the plants.' I stop, exhausted by saying so much about my life.

'You are a good man. Will you come to Baguio?'

'Yes.'

She wraps herself around me and hugs me tight. Outside the sky finally cracks open: thunder and then the downpour.

It is less humid in North Luzon. The skyline is like a children's picture, ranges of mountains get darker and bluer into the distance.

There is a scent everywhere that Consuela tells me is pine and something called frangipani. It's a bit of a change from the sooty, dusty smells of Manila.

'Baguio was the summer capital of the Philippines,' Consuela tells me.

The cottages that we see from the taxi on the journey from the airport look the part, hiding amongst pine trees, a cross between Swiss chalets and those Chinese pagodas, I think. Baguio is modern. The Yanks built it at the beginning of the century, but it had to be rebuilt when the Japs and Jerries had finished with it after the War. The streets have tall white or peach-coloured buildings, square, with balconies. There are billboards everywhere, of every size, screaming with every clashing colour you can think of, so that the place looks cluttered and permanently on the go. On the high lampposts that splay at the top to light both sides of the road there are big yellow plastic daisies hanging down, ridiculous looking.

The Luz family live in a street near the centre of the city, amongst a rambling jumble of apartments that seem to be full of Consuela's cousins, aunts and uncles. I'm dizzy with the names before we ever get to meet Consuela's parents.

'Jim Vaughan, this is my mother, Isabella Luz and my father, Antonio Luz,' Consuela says with a formality that can't hide her grin. I think she might be about to break into song or dance.

I hold out my hand to shake theirs. They look older than me, but it can't be by much. I've been in the sun so long they're not much darker than me. The father has a long face, long nose, almost European looking, but I remember there were a lot of Spanish about at one time. I'm grateful for the cooler air here, more like an English summer. At least my palms are dry when we shake hands.

'You are very welcome, Jim,' Isabella says. 'You make Consuela very happy.'

She's shorter than Consuela, more rounded features. Consuela is more like her dad, I think – a softened version. I relax, madly grateful that they have not barraged me with interrogation about what I'm doing with their daughter or begun screaming at me in Filipino. I survey the crowd around me, not unlike a family gathering when one of Cath's sisters gets married, children everywhere, the smells of cooking and noises of an overcrowded family. We are the last to arrive before they can begin to eat and they know how to put on a spread. There's pork, of course, and other meat dishes with fruit mixed in, pineapple mostly, and jugs of kalamansi juice with soda. The strawberries that Consuela told me about look too small, but they taste as sweet as any in England.

In the evening we walk to Burnham Park for the Independence Day fireworks, Isabella and Antonio hand in hand in front of us, married for longer than me and Cath, still holding hands, the way we never did. Cath wouldn't have that in public. I slip my hand into Consuela's and we stay like that, walking, gazing at the sky for the display to begin. Thirty-two years with Cath, the girls grown up, Megan's life going on as if I don't exist. I squeeze Consuela's hand in mine. She has long cool fingers with dry skin that is more used to work than I would like. I know, as the first enormous firework cracks into a gold shower that hides the stars, that we do not have thirty-two years ahead of us. The fireworks light up the big central lake that takes up a lot of the park, the rowing boats with swans heads and plastic awnings hung with plastic flowers are moored at one side of the lake. On the way back to Consuela's parents' house it begins to rain. Soft mountain rain that reminds me of home, hardly visible at first, a mist of drops that looks like nothing and soaks to the marrow. I wonder what Megan is doing now.

We are tourists again for the next few days; visiting places in the mountains around Baguio as though it is all new to Consuela; packing the sights into our short stay as though it's just a taster and we will return again and again to make these places familiar, a part of who we will become together, but I know it won't be like that. I concentrate as we rush around, commit things to memory: Camp John Hay where some Jap general surrendered to a Yank at the end of the War, Wainwright I think he was called. I can't fix the Japanese name in my head. Now the place has one of those leisure centres and a golf course. We borrow a car from Consuela's brother, Ernesto, thirty-nine and married with children that I never manage to count properly. Four, I think.

The Ambuklao reservoir up in the mountains goes on for miles, much bigger than Tanygrisiau Dam where I used to take the girls for picnics, Cath refusing to come and sit on the benches in case they might be dirty. Higher up, the pine forests thicken, it is even cooler up there. Fresh. The wet-rice terraces are something to see: mountain sides cut into flat steps so that the mountains look man-made, almost like pyramids. They have irrigation channels and some of the terraces are walled with stones that seem to bend in around the top. Marvellous when you think about it. We visit a place called Banuo, a scruffy town that looks more like something out of a Wild West film, tall wooden or plasterboard buildings, shacks on stilts, some with red or green roofs. Reminds me of taking Cath to the flicks.

Beyond Banuo, the mountains are scattered with little clumps of housing, seven or ten together – huts really, but with carvings on them that must take some doing.

'They are Ifugao,' Consuela explains. 'they are Malay like all people here before the Spanish.'

'The originals then?'

'Ah, before them there were pygmies and such.'

'Like the beaker people.'

'Beaker people, Jim?'

'They were in Britain before the Celts. Seems to be the way of islands, eh? Always someone new.'

Consuela smiles and nods. 'Always someone new, Jim. They almost died out in the War, but there are more again now. The government have programmes to help the Ifugao.'

'Like a protected species,' I offer. 'What's growing lower down, near the houses?'

'Sweet potatoes. Most of the rice is sold, but the sweet potatoes are what people live on.'

The rice looks like it is growing in shallow pools, a kind of pale lime colour poking through the water. 'And the pigs and chickens?'

'Yes, a little, for feasts, but they are mostly used for sacrifices.'

'Sacrifices? They're not Catholics then?'

'The Ifugao have their own beliefs, more than a thousand gods, and they worship Ancestors. The gods are called on for everything: illness or troubles. There is lots of feasting, lots of rice wine too. The Spanish missionaries did their best to change things, but these beliefs are very old. Even those who are Catholic have many other beliefs.'

'I've noticed,' I say, thinking of Consuela's refusal to live in a house with six steps, her many superstitions and insistence on luck that reminds me constantly of my mam.

'So these sacrifices, were they ever human?'

'No, Jim! But the people here used to hunt heads.'

It sounds barbaric, but I've heard that about the Celts too, though I couldn't tell you whether it's true or not, and of course English Kings chopped enough heads off, let alone what they did to the Welsh. We're not much different the world over when you think about it: brutal and superstitious, doing whatever it takes to get a good crop or to save a child from burning up with fever.

Gastroenteritis, it was. Not a word I'll ever forget. I remember standing in the living room in Blaenau, the doctor holding onto Megan, bawling in his arms, red faced and flushed.

'I have to get her to hospital, Mr Vaughan. It's very urgent. Your baby is very dehydrated. She's very sick. If you get in my way she could die.'

Cath sits on the sofa, not crying, shut down. Her eyes are circled with dark and sinking into her face.

'The filthy hospital's where she got this from in the first place!' My voice cracks with tears and fury, hoarse and loud. I don't normally raise my voice like this, especially not to doctors. The sound of my own voice makes me dizzy. I won't let him take Megan back to that place. Five babies born on that ward are already dead. She is two weeks old. We've only had her at home for a few days, four days I think.

'I'm afraid there does seem to be a link between this outbreak and a particular ward, Mr Vaughan. It's very unfortunate, but the affected ward has been shut down and there will be a full enquiry. Your baby will be in a completely different unit, Mr Vaughan. We must get fluids into her if she is to fight this thing.'

'I'll feed her fluids. I'll stay up night and day, whatever it takes.' I know I'm clutching at straws, but I can't just give in.

'She can't keep anything down Mr Vaughan. She has to be put on a drip. It could save her life.'

'Could save her life? Could? What do you mean, "could"?'

123

'Mr Vaughan, I really don't have time. You must let me take her.'

'No!'

I scream, cry, beat on the wall. Behind me, Cath says, 'Take the baby, Dr Kerr, I'll see to him.'

'No!' But I don't stop him, just sink down the living room wall and howl. If I'd had gods they could have had all the rice wine and pigs in the world to save Megan. I got her back, of course, but I envy these people the feeling that they can do something, even if it isn't true.

Consuela is telling me more about history and the different people, '...part of the Igorot peoples. Lower down, in the rain forests there are groups that grow dry rice in gardens that move with the seasons and some Gaddang live in tree houses still. The Igorot peoples are skilled metalworkers, iron and brass, even some gold and they weave – baskets and blankets. They all believe in spirits, and ancestors...'

I nod as though I'm really listening.

'Are you alright, Jim? You look pale.'

I put an arm round her and pull her to me.

'Never been better.'

We develop a kind of routine back in Manila: my work; Consuela's quilts. There are storms in the winter. In November one of them works itself into a typhoon out in the bay, swirling at over seventy miles an hour, but it spends itself before it can do much damage. Only the squatters camped in makeshift shacks have to rebuild. There are earth tremors too that turn my stomach at first, but it's strange what you can get used to, even eating mangoes for breakfast instead of bacon.

Consuela and I have coughs in the winter and I insist we get checked out for TB, which is rife here. But it's only the pollution, the cough everyone in Manila shares. The thought of TB scratches at my memory. The TB hospital is where Cath and me both worked, where we met that autumn, in a place with cold days, gold leaves and a sky so blue it made your eyes water to look. In Manila it is hot, then wet; dry, then wet. The air is always heavy with thunder, noise and filth.

I picture Cath outside the TB hospital. She has the most gorgeous red hair tied back in a high pony tail. She is wearing a blue skirt that hugs her hips and a pale blue blouse that follows her shape.

I'm thinking: I'll take that girl to the pictures. Then it comes to me: I'm going to marry that girl.

I watch Consuela standing in our white kitchen, marinating pork, washing rice for stones, the dry cough catching in her throat. She has hair like dark silk, a waterfall of hair caught in a red tie at the back of her neck. I think: I love this girl. Then it comes to me: there's no future in it.

Maybe it is *mukha*. I've learned to live the Filipino way or maybe it's just how I am, not saying what I want, not contradicting, saying yes when I mean no to save face or because I'm weak, but how can I tell her? I didn't tell Cath after thirty-two years of marriage, I sent her a note.

'We will be together forever, Jim?'

'Yes.'

'Maybe we could move to Baguio one day? You liked it there?'

'Yes.'

'I am so happy, Jim, and you are happy?'

'Yes.'

125

Maybe Consuela knows. She is used to living with *mukha*. They say yes here rather than disagree, but it is understood that it is politeness, saving face, not the truth, whatever that might be. Maybe I was just born to make a bloody mess.

On the morning of my fifty-fifth birthday the water is off in the house. We lose power and water on and off, but today Consuela has planned a feast. She smiles to cover her disappointment. We catch a taxi to the bay. The sand is white, a thin strip of it hemmed in by palms, tropical trees and bushes. The air is already sticky, but it's a bit lighter here by the shore. Out in the bay we watch container ships and closer in the fishing boats, moored for the day, their outriders like the legs of water boatmen, some with long, triangular sails. The sky is changing all the time. Moody, Megan would call it, but we can see just beyond the Manila skyline to the dark blue shapes of mountains. I want to take it all in.

We go to a mall where I drink kalamansi juice with soda and Consuela has diet coke, no ice. I long for ice, but Consuela says that freezing does not purify the water, only boiling.

By the time we get back, a snail's pace through the jungle of Manila traffic, the water is back on and Consuela sets about her feast.

'Jim,' Consuela says softly.

'Eh? Sorry, Cariad, I just shut my eyes for forty winks, must've dozed off.'

Consuela slides onto the couch next to me. She has a tiny parcel in her hands. 'This is for you, Jim.'

I open it carefully, peeling away the tiny bow and precisely folded gold paper. I have never worn a ring before.

'It is gold from the mountains, from the Igorot people,' Consuela says, smiling while she bites her bottom lip with a touch of anxiety. 'Do you like it, Jim?'

'It's fantastic, of course I like it.'

We both smile.

We eat the meal, a chicken dish. Consuela wanted to buy fish, but it's a red tide, so she says the fish can't be trusted. Afterwards, Consuela takes my hand across the table.

'I have another present, Jim.'

I look around.

'Not that kind.' She smiles, her voice not much more than a whisper. I wonder if it is something that will happen in the bedroom and wish I'd eaten less.

'I think I am...I mean I am...' Her eyes look slightly moist and my skin begins to prickle in the silence. 'I am going to have our baby, Jim.'

It lies between us in the silence, slippery as a newborn. I watch her, her dark eyes are wide, as humid as the skies outside waiting to crack with thunder.

'Are you pleased, Jim?' She says in the end. She is flushed, her eyes blink back fear.

'Yes. Yes, of course.' I smile and squeeze both her hands in mine.

What else could I say?

At work next day I write the note: over and over, filling the waste basket with the office's thick, cream sheets of watermarked paper. There is no airmail paper here; it would probably not survive the heat, thin pages soggy with humidity tearing at a touch, so we have this thick, expensive paper, vellum I think it's called. What can I say? In the end, I make it simple, eleven words to end what has taken two years, the first six months in

Algie, what seems like a lifetime ago, the rest here in this other world where I will never belong: *'Dear Consuela, I have to go home. All my love, Jim.'*

I make a call to the airport, go to the bank at lunch time, leave work as though it's just another day, eat the meal Consuela has cooked me, with the money and the note burning a hole in my mind all evening.

Consuela is a deep sleeper, the sign of an easy conscience, my mam always said. I move around the room like a cat, collect a few shirts, silk creasing into the little case or cotton, stiffer and easier to fold in the dark, while Consuela sleeps with our baby growing inside her.

It is Tuesday tomorrow, Consuela will leave early to go to the market at Greenbelt Park. I'll pretend to go to work, come back in when the house is empty, pick up the little case that I've pushed beneath the bed, check my passport and leave the fat, cream envelope bulging with money and the note. I'll be at Nikoy Aquino two hours before my flight, just as Consuela is arriving home with fruit and fresh herbs.

I don't go straight home, or even straight to Megan. I find a run-down hotel in one of the streets off Waterloo station. Megan is just a few miles away, Elin is somewhere a bit further out, in North-West London, working in an office doing her husband's paperwork. I imagine Cath back at home, in the house in Bangor that she insisted we buy after I got the job in Algeria.

I need some time. Just a few days, I tell myself, time to take it all in, to give myself a breather between two worlds. I'll take a few days.

It's over six weeks by the time I wake up one morning and know it has to be now. I check out of the hotel and find a hire car place half-way across London. I'll need to drive to Bangor, but I'll go to Megan's first. Megan will know what to do.

The first time I drive past Megan's house, I think I will be sick on the spot. I go to a pub to pull myself together, drive past again, force myself to pull over, get out of the car and knock.

There is no answer. All the houses here look empty – working couples, hardly any children around. By the time I drive back it is dark. There is a light on, shining through the drawn curtains, but it's too late in the day. I want to be able to talk to Megan without that clown of an English husband hanging round.

I feel like death warmed up after a night in the car. 4am: it's too early to wake Megan. I find a workmen's caff near the Rotherhithe tunnel, a bit of a dump, but it will do. A middle-aged woman with greasy hair pulled back from a sharp face sidles over to my table. The Formica top is covered in tea stains, some old and ingrained, some dried on. Cath would never eat here, I think. The woman flicks a grey dishcloth over the table surface.

'What can I get you, ducks?' She has ugly teeth when she smiles.

'Tea, please.' I feel suddenly hungry. 'Are you doing breakfast?'

'Full English?'

I nod. The red plastic seat underneath me is ripped and I can feel the sharp edges. The tea is thick and bitter, I reckon you could stand a spoon in it. The green mug has a chip, stained almost black. There's plenty of food: two sausages, two eggs, bacon, toast, tinned tomatoes. I pick at it, losing my appetite with every mouthful. I stir plenty of sugar into the tea, to try to take away the bitterness, but it doesn't help. It is still only 4.30. I leave the food, leave money on the table and go back to the car.

What have I done?

When I picture Consuela, I know why I did it. She's brown and soft and doesn't say no like Cath, but all the same I could never stop thinking about home: the grey streets and grey slag tips, the Moelwyns and the rain, the way a cup of tea tastes with a fat bacon sandwich on a winter morning. We live with all these dreams. I wish I could start it all again.

Monday 16th July

The rain starts as they turn into Megan's street.

'Just in time,' Megan says, rubbing her arms free of the few plump raindrops that have settled on her.

'Wasn't expecting rain today,' Jim says, grateful for something to talk about.

They duck into the tiny hallway of Megan's house as the rain speeds up.

'Like this all the bloody time in this country,' Cath says, sourly. 'Forgotten what it's like after eighteen months in the sun, have you?'

'I'll just nip to the bathroom,' Jim says.

'I'll make his life such hell when I get him home, he'll regret he was ever born.'

'What's the point in that, Mam?'

'What's the point? You can be very stupid for such an intelligent person, Megan. Don't know why you keep on taking his side after all he's done.'

'I just meant...' Megan trails away, listens to her dad's slow steps coming downstairs.

'Got the place nice up there, Megan. I like a bit of blue, very restful.'

'We're not here to discuss Megan's decorating. Sit down.'

Jim folds himself into the armchair.

'So it's about time you told me what you think you're playing at.'

'Don't know what you mean, Love.'

Megan sits on the sofa at the opposite end to her mother and sighs. It's not yet two o'clock. Ben won't be home until six or seven this evening.

'I'll give you "don't know what you mean, Love",' Cath apes Jim's voice badly. 'I want some answers. Now. How old was the black tart?'

Jim shrugs, avoids eye contact.

'I said how old was the black tart?' Cath is flushed now.

'Mam...'

'Shut up, Megan. Jim?'

Jim shrugs again, hunches into himself.

'Of course you bloody know. Tell me. Ten years younger than you? Fifteen years younger than you?' Cath is shouting now. 'Filthy black whore, don't know where they've been, people like that.'

'That's enough, Cath.'

'I'll say when it's enough. How old did you say she was?'

'I didn't,' Jim says through gritted teeth.

'Probably been on the game since she was twelve. Isn't that what they're like in those places, mothers sell them off when there's not enough work in the paddy fields, don't they?'

'That's enough!' Jim stands up, paces the too-cramped room. He won't give Consuela away. 'That's enough,' he repeats quietly. He turns to Megan. 'How about another cup of tea, Cariad? Your mam could do with a drink.'

Outside the sky darkens, the plump summer rain grows torrential.

'Must've brought one of those monsoons back with you,' Cath hisses. 'Just hope it's all you've brought, hope there's nothing else catching.'

Jim sighs and slumps back into the chair, head in his hands. In the kitchen he can hear the sounds of Megan making tea. What is Consuela doing now?

The tremors start early, the tiny judders that no-one notices at first. Consuela smoothes the thick white cotton sheet across the double bed in the Baguio hotel where she works as a maid. She eases upright and lays a hand on her stomach. Fifteen weeks. Six weeks since Jim left, no, seven weeks tomorrow. Her hand goes to the little silver necklace that she never takes off, an open heart with a horseshoe inside. The room flickers again, a tremor so small that Consuela wonders if it is her own eyesight. Does pregnancy affect eyesight? She is almost finished. She will be home soon, back to her parents' home in time for breakfast with her father before he heads to the mine. In another room, her mother, Isabella, is making an identical bed. They can walk home together, rest for a while before the next half of the shift they work.

Consuela wonders if Jim is asleep. It is what? Eight hours behind? Or is it different in summer? Seven hours behind, almost one in the morning.

It is an ordinary day without Jim, the baby growing inside her, though hardly noticeable yet.

The quake comes suddenly, half an hour after Consuela and Isabella begin the second half of their shift. They are not together. Consuela looks up from the wreckage of the broken concrete staircase. She can hear screaming, see daylight where a wall should be, where her mother had gone ahead just a few minutes before. Her right leg is trapped by debris and she retches at the sharpness of the pain when she tries to dislodge it. She can't see any blood. She feels her face and head, covered in concrete and plaster dust that clogs her nose and throat. She passes a hand over her stomach which feels the same, leans forward and

133

begins dislodging the smaller shards of rubble below her knee. The plush lobby below her is a mêlée of concrete and glass, as though the front wall has fallen in on itself. There are no doors, no exits, the reception desk is buried under thick slabs of concrete and Consuela thinks she can hear a faint whimpering sound. The section of stairs that she was climbing appears to be suspended on a bed of rubble. Not far above her, where the staircase recently bent round ninety degrees to the right, there is a gap, a drop into who knows what. She concentrates on the fragments of concrete, pushing steadily at a larger slab. It dislodges suddenly, but not from her efforts. The precarious wreckage of staircase tilts. Consuela hears her own thin scream like something faraway and unreal as she catches sight of her fractured leg, a piece of bone jutting through muscle and blood above the ankle. A dislocated wedge of concrete skims over her, glances her forehead with a dull crack on its way past. She reaches towards the sticky stream of blood and gasps.

It is almost five o'clock. In another world it is nine o'clock in the morning.

Jim sits in Megan's living room while his daughter goes for an ante-natal appointment. His wife will be with him soon. His pregnant mistress is closing her eyes and losing consciousness.

'Nice cup of tea, Pet,' Jim says.

He looks up at his daughter and she smiles. Cath is silent. He glances at the clock. Three o'clock on the longest day of his life.

It takes the volunteers six hours to hack through the first pile of hotel wreckage that has bulged out into the street. The city is cut off, emergency help could take forty-eight hours or more, Antonio has heard, and the hospital is damaged.

They've been told to take the wounded, or the bodies, to tents set up outside the hospital, far enough away to escape debris from aftershocks. They are a strange crew, Antonio thinks, a bunch of his colleagues with mining picks, some army cadets led by a drill sergeant.

Three of the hotels have come down, but this one is where Isabella and Consuela work. He has heard that there is a fire at the factory where his oldest son, Ernesto works, that there are men trapped in there, but he can't think about that now. Isabella is in there, Isabella who he has loved since he was fifteen years old and Consuela, their late baby, who has bad luck, who he worships.

They work with hardly a rest, grateful for the overcast sky, hacking away or carrying debris in grim silence except for the shouts of order or advice. They have only picks and their hands to work with. After six hours they have their first glimpse of what used to be the sleek hotel lobby where the most affluent summer tourists arrived: Americans, Australians and Germans, rich Chinese from Hong Kong. A wreck of a recently grand staircase spills into view and there is someone there, a girl, a young woman. The workers scrabble more frantically through the shattered lumps of concrete, ears pricked for aftershocks, bodies tense with the sight of someone almost within reach, someone very still, covered in pale concrete dust, twisted at an odd angle across the remains of several steps.

Antonio uses his pick to carefully ease a slab forward, to widen the space enough to get someone inside. A young cadet is at his side.

'Let me,' he says simply and is gone through the gap. Antonio watches. The cadet, his short hair spiked with sweat from six hours of digging with his bare hands, his fatigues plastered in dust, lifts chunks of concrete from around the figure. A face lolls backwards into view and Antonio freezes. He sinks down as other volunteers rush towards him, he doesn't hear his own cries, he doesn't know that he is shaking, kneeling in the dust, wailing over and over: 'Consuela! Consuela!' as her limp body is freed, passed through the gap as though it is some sacred relic.

'Suppose you're thinking about your little black tart?' Cath spits into the silent, uneasy room.

Jim only shrugs, takes another mouthful of tea, and closes his eyes.

'So — you going to tell me anything?'

Jim shrugs again.

'Do you see? Do you see what I have to put up with? I suppose you're still siding with him, after all he's put me through. Coming back here as if he's just been to the corner shop for a paper.'

'It's not a matter of sides, Mam. You don't have to go home together.'

'Oh, so I'm supposed to let him get away with it, am I? Oh no, he's coming home. He's going to suffer for what he's done.'

'I'm going to have a lie down. You two should have some time to yourselves and I'm exhausted.'

Jim gets up as Megan moves towards the living room door.

'Sorry about this, Pet. You're alright, aren't you? The baby and everything?'

'I'm fine, Dad, I just need a rest.'

In the Silence

Megan shuts the door to her bedroom, stands with her back to it for a moment, sighs, and moves to the bed. She pulls off her shoes, allows the print cotton skirt to fall on the blue carpet, stretches out on the quilt, coils back into a foetal curl and closes her eyes.

She can picture the last time she saw the yellow bedroom.

Her mother never comes into her room now. She leaves laundry and clean sheets outside the room, as she has for almost three years since Tada began working abroad in a country she can hardly imagine. He works three months on, two weeks off. When he is at home he is quiet and distant. Once he brought her a sand rose and another time a scorpion, its tail raised for the sting, frozen in resin. A paperweight, he said, but he doesn't talk about Algeria.

When he is at home he waits up for Megan when she is out late with Ben. He doesn't say anything about Ben either, a Londoner studying Economics and Social Policy at Bangor.

Cath tries to goad Ben with jibes that he can't understand. 'Dim gwerth rhech dafad,' she says when he tells her what she's studying.

'Not worth a sheep's fart,' Megan translates later, but they agree Cath is not worth arguing with. When Megan finishes her A-levels Cath charges her rent: fourteen pounds a week of Megan's fourteen pounds and forty pence. Megan hands it over. She eats a slice of toast at home in the morning, then goes to Ben's flat. It's expensive toast, hard not to play Cath's game, to spit out some comment, but she won't play.

'I want you in by nine o'clock in future.' Cath announces.

'Pardon?'

'Don't you "pardon" me. I don't know what you might be getting up to with your filthy boyfriend, out all hours.'

Elin skitters away from the breakfast table with a slice of toast in her hand. She is thirteen, quiet – too quiet, and her eyes are permanently hooded. She is bullied at school, but Cath won't talk to the teachers about it. She says it will only make things worse. She keeps Elin at home several days each week, Megan notices, telling her that not everyone needs to be clever. In the holidays Elin never sees friends.

'Whatever you like,' Megan says, leaving the dining room after Elin.

'Pardon?' Cath calls after her.

Megan resists the urge to parrot: 'don't you "pardon" me'.

'Bye, see you tonight,' She calls from the front door and exits quickly, catches the bus with the money Ben gives her. She will wait in his house until he is home from work, clean up for him and his flat-mate, Ryan. When she's finished she will read novels in the little garden.

Megan is home by nine. She goes to her room, moves around quietly. After three days she is ready. There is not much.

'I won't be home tonight, Mam.'

'What did you say to me?'

Elin picks up her toast, leaves the room. It is Saturday morning in late August, two days after Megan

139

has picked up her A-level results. Her English teacher, Mr White, took her and the two other 'A' grade students out for drinks on the night of the results. Her mother made a sour face and said nothing.

'I said I won't be coming home today, Mam.' Megan glances through the side window. The stained glass throws a rainbow across the dining room table. At the end of the driveway she sees Ben pull up in his newly acquired car, old and loved.

'I'm moving out today. I'm going to stay with Ben and Ryan till I go to university.'

'You're what?' Cath gets up and raises a fist, but stands motionless.

Cath stamps upstairs, slams into the bathroom.

Megan walks upstairs quietly. In the bedroom everything is packed, the wardrobe stacked inside with a few boxes, her clothes in bin liners under the bed. She carries the bags and boxes to Ben at the front door. On her last trip to the bedroom her mother is there, looking out of the window, watching Ben load Megan's few items into his car. Megan picks up her patchwork bag from where it lies on the yellow nylon bed-cover.

'I'm going now, Mam.'

Cath turns her back. 'Good riddance then, and don't come crying to me when he dumps you on the streets or when you catch something dirty.'

'Bye, Mam.'

Megan turns to leave and her mother moves towards her. 'All these bloody years I've fed and clothed you and for what? So that you can go off to university and then make money for that waste of time.'

'Pardon?'

'I've brought you up. I'm the one who should benefit from your education, not him.'

Megan turns and leaves.

Megan hears her mother shout obscenities as she reaches the front door for the last time, but she doesn't turn around. Ben puts an arm around her, holds her for a moment before they walk down the drive together.

The decision to marry before university is a sudden one, but Ben is happy with the suggestion. They are engaged anyway and Megan knows that he fears losing her once she is so far away. They have four weeks to the date Megan wants. She writes to her tada in Algeria, but there is no reply. Megan phones the house, but Cath hangs up. She waits outside school for Elin one evening, but misses her, or perhaps Elin isn't at school that day.

Two days before she leaves for Cambridge, Megan Vaughan is gone, replaced by Megan Ashley.

She doesn't see her parents for eighteen months, but Jim finally calls when he comes home on leave. Elin is fifteen. 'Nervous breakdown or something...' Jim says down the telephone line, '...It'd do her good to see you, Megan.'

'You're well out of it,' Elin confides.

Megan is surprised when Elin breaks away from home four years later and marries Terry. But since Jim went absent without leave Cath has moved into Elin's life again. She persuades Elin that she couldn't cope with children, pays for the private sterilisation that Terry doesn't know about until it is too late. Elin looks thin and quiet again, but maybe she and Terry will have a chance now that Cath is leaving. Megan feels ill at ease about her pregnancy when she is with Terry and Elin.

Megan rouses to the sound of raised voices downstairs. She covers her face with a pillow and tries to shut out the sounds, or at least the words. She falls asleep to the drone of argument, as she has so many times, wakes feeling groggy and dehydrated.

Megan tiptoes to the bathroom, splashes her face and runs a glass of cool water. She holds the glass to her temples after she has drunk the water, then refills it. It is quiet downstairs. Megan wonders if her parents have gone out, but it is still raining outside. She makes her way back to the blue bedroom. She wonders about doing some work, but decides that the day has been lost, it is almost five o'clock. She lies back on the bed and reaches for the novel she is reading. An hour or two and Ben will be home.

Cath and Jim are exhausted. Cath spits an occasional insult, but otherwise they are silent.

I've never been travel sick in my life, but I feel ill all the way home on the plane from Manila, thinking about Consuela. I wonder when she will read the note. She might not go into the bedroom straight away, it could be hours. She might sit in the living room worrying when I don't come home, maybe phone the emergency services, before she picks up the note. I should have left the note and money in the kitchen, on the table. I should have told her to her face that I had to go, but how could I?

I turn the gold ring on my finger, the only ring I've ever worn: gold from the mines near Consuela's home in Baguio, plaited into a ring by one of the many jewellers in the city. I will have to take it off before Cath sees it. I can feel acid rising, my guts tensing. If I could have Consuela and be back at home. If I could have Consuela and not lose Megan. If I could have Consuela and feel no guilt about Cath. I close my eyes.

I picture our rented house in Fort Bonoficio: the high walls, the bars on the windows, the security guard outside since I started to work for the American firm, the cardboard mat at the door soaked with Baygon poison to ward off the dengue mosquitoes.

Inside there are mosquito shades at all the windows and mosquito coils to burn. The water and power go off from time to time, even in this ex-pat area. Despite all of Consuela's precautions I come down with a higad rash; the spikes of the venomous caterpillar brush on my hand from a mango that hasn't been washed yet. Consuela soaks my hand in calamine lotion while it blows up and itches, red and angry under the dry white coating that makes me look like a corpse. How can people live here? It is not a place where I can belong.

The night that Consuela tells me about the baby I don't sleep. I get up and pace the living room; the way I used to pace the landing after Mam died. There is no one to turn to. Megan is miles away. The child will be a stranger to me, a foreigner from a foreign place, a child that smiles and says yes in that way that always includes no; a child that knows, without having to remind himself over and over, about *mukha*; who counts steps without thinking about it, sees chi and spirits everywhere and lights candles in churches to beg Catholic saints for good luck. The child will be Filipino, not my child.

143

Consuela is a dream: she will always be a dream, like the beautiful women in the movies when I was young. I'm fool. If I'd just left her as the dream, not grasped after her until she became too real. I have always wanted a son. I have always wanted a beautiful woman who says yes, but now that these things are there in front of me they are not what I imagined.

Consuela tells me a story one day. 'In the Bible, Jim, there is a parable that Jesus tells about a father with two sons. One son is good and compliant, he always says yes to whatever his father commands, but he doesn't always do the thing, only says it. The other son is disrespectful: he says he will not do as he is told, and yet he does what his father asks, even after saying no. In the Bible, Jesus asks his followers who is the good son and the right answer is supposed to be the second son, Jim, but this is strange to us. Filipinos are like the first son: we say yes, it is impolite to say no – we might lose face, or the person asking might lose face. It is always best to say yes whatever you intend, Jim. A good life is not to break *mukha*. We are surprised that Jesus did not understand this, but he was not Filipino. You understand?'

I understand. Consuela is brown and soft and always says yes. She is my dream but she is not my dream. I understand that I will never understand.

So I sit on a plane, feeling sick, worrying about what I have done, thinking about Consuela who I will always love, and my son.

In the hotel in London – the place is too seedy to call a hotel – I have a lot of time to think about things. I've always worked with men – at the mine, in Algeria, but everything has always revolved around women: mother, wife, daughters, and now a mistress.

*

I am Mam's favourite. Later, she has a soft spot for Carri, the baby. But growing up, I'm her favourite.

'I think our Jim's broken a leg, Mam.' I can hear Hugh, fifteen, big boned and hard voiced booming through the little window at the back of the shop.

'What? Where is he?'

'In the back yard. He jumped off the shed.'

'What? Stay here, Hugh, watch the shop for me.'

'But Mam, I'll be late for work. Mr Jones says...'

'Never mind what Mr Jones. Just watch this shop if you don't want a clip round the ear.'

'Yes, Mam.'

I imagine Hugh dipping his hand into a jar of rosie apples that Mam has been about to screw shut and put back on the shelf after the last customer. If Hugh jumped off the shed roof she'd clip him round the ear. I bite my lip against the pain. I try to think about the tart tang of the rosie apples that make me blink as fast as pain. I hear Mam come into the yard that runs behind the shop and down the side of our house.

'Menna! Menna, run and fetch Doctor Griffiths.'

Mam leans over me. 'You're soft in the head, Edwin James Vaughan,' she says. She leans over me.

'I thought I could fly, Mam, like Mary Poppins.'

'Just lie still. Menna won't be long fetching Doctor Griffiths, Cariad.'

She draws a hand through my hair. I can smell the sweets on her hands, the sticky lick of sugar over the comforting smell of her cigarette smoke.

'I'll get you a blanket while we're waiting.'

'No, it's alright. Just stay here, Mam.' I grab her hand as she makes a movement away. She puts an arm round me and I lean into her, the smells of cigarette smoke and sweets wraps itself round me better than a blanket.

In hospital, after they've opened her up, Mam looks wizened. Her skin has lost its moisture all at once, dried up like a raisin. Her blue eyes have lost their sharpness; they already look milky, far away.

Menna is at her side, holding her hand. She looks ill herself, her skin sinking into her big round face, the eye sockets too large, but I don't know then that she is getting ready to follow Mam. She doesn't know it herself, or if she does, she doesn't say anything. Alun is at the end of the bed, clutching on to the cold metal rail as though he might fall if he lets go.

His eyes have all Mam's blue, but watered down at the moment, red-rimmed. Dad and Hugh huddle at the far side of the room, talking in low voices.

'I thought she was being moved to convalescence tomorrow. I don't understand,' I say quietly.

There is a trace of a sneer on Hugh's face. 'Don't talk soft, that's just what they say.'

'What?'

He lowers his voice further. 'When they open someone up and take one look and then close them up again, Jim: it means there's nothing they can do. She must have known about this for months, longer even.'

'What?'

'For Christ's sake, Jim; she's riddled with it. You don't get better and she must have been putting up with it for ages. You know what she's like, she never did like doctors.'

My dad paces about like a trapped bear, forcing back tears.

I move round to Mam's other side, take her other hand and Menna gives me a weak smile across the bed.

Afterwards, when we've stopped crying, or at least paused, we gaze at each other in the corridor as though we're not sure who the others are for a moment. Then the flood breaks and we stand in the corridor blubbing, noisy tears running with snot, holding onto each other and rocking with the storm of it while Dad, Hugh and Alun move away.

It's not something I can control: the sleep, the crying. I hate Megan reading that Bible. Bloody God, what difference does he make? But Mam gave her the Bible, taught her the psalm off by heart when she was seven: *The Lord is my Shepherd.* The one we mumble together at the funeral in the cold chapel and I have to believe Mam's not gone, not completely gone, even when I don't believe it. How can I? She's not there. My mam's not there and it feels like the whole world should explode with the grief of it, but it all goes on as though nothing has happened. The cars still work, night still follows day and the more normal it all is, the worse things feel. I can't believe Cath can still write shopping lists, Megan can still read her books, Elin can still pull the heads off her dolls with a grin on her face.

I can't believe I still know how to get dressed and go to work, but it's not all normal. I can't sleep anymore and I can't stop crying.

Cath says Elin has nightmares. I don't think she does, but it means that she can take Elin into her room at night, keep me out. It doesn't make much difference, she's always kept me out anyway, but I want my mam. I want to be held. I want my mam. Up and down the stairs, back and forth across the landing, holding

147

myself, my own arms wrapped round me, standing in the dark rocking and crying, Mam, Mam, Mam!

I hear Megan moving at night sometimes. She reads her books late with just that little lamp my mam gave her. Sometimes she has nosebleeds and has to sit on the edge of her bed, head forward, pinching hard at the flow of blood till it stops. I can't stand the sight of blood.

There's one night when she creeps to the bathroom, the small squeak of her door, the tiny pad of her bare feet across the carpet, just the moon lighting the landing through the side window. I should have realised it would be a nosebleed, a bad one if she goes to the bathroom, but I'm dizzy with loneliness and crying. I want to see her, small and soft in her white nightdress, red hair plaited, but dishevelled from being in bed so that it wisps round her little face, green eyes looking at me as though I'm someone worth seeing. In the bathroom she is leaning over the sink, her back to me. I still don't think about what must be happening,

I move up close and there it is: the blood, big drops of it exploding on the white porcelain. She turns at the moment I register the blood, steps towards me as I fall into her. When I come round, the blood has blobbed into my blue pyjamas and I feel faint again, but the nosebleed has stopped. Megan is pinned under my weight, awkward and shivering, but I can still feel some warmth in her, some softness despite how thin and small she seems.

'Mam,' I say, and the tears start again, fat and silent.

'Tada, are you alright, Tada? I thought you'd...' Megan's voice is full of fear for me. She'd care if I dropped down dead, she'd feel the weight of the world on her like I do for my mam. She is so small, only eight, but she understands things Cath never will. She understands like my mam.

That's all I was thinking. I tell her to keep quiet. I only wanted somewhere to find some comfort. And she seems alright. She's happy with Ben, good at her job, a clever girl with a nice house and a baby on the way. Megan's alright.

I hate the thought of going abroad, but there's no other work and Cath won't settle in that council house in Tanygrisiau.

I don't mean to meet Consuela, but there she is, with her smile and saying yes, always saying yes.

In Baguio we borrow a car from Ernesto. He is fourteen years older than Consuela, the oldest of three boys, the other two born quickly after one another, Rodriguez and Antonio, then a ten year gap before the baby, the only girl: Consuela. They are bound to be protective. I think how I would feel if someone twenty years older was living with Carri.

Ernesto hands me the car keys and shows me how things work, he smiles all the time, little circular nods that could include yes or no as he speaks, but he never quite looks me in the eye. He leaves me to load our small suitcases while he fetches Consuela. She comes down after a while with the whole family to wave us off.

In the car Consuela bites her lip and looks at me sideways. Her hands have a way of moving in her lap when she is thinking about something, a small rubbing motion.

'Everything okay?'

She smiles and nods. I lean over and take one hand loosely in mine, squeeze and set her palm down on my knee. 'Nice to have a trip out,' I say to ease the silence.

Consuela smiles, nods, the same movement that Ernesto makes, that they all make.

'Sure everything's alright?'

Consuela bites her lip harder and shuffles in the cramped car seat to face me. 'Ernesto, my brother, he is only concerned for me.'

'Because of me?'

'Because I am his sister and they think I am still the baby.'

'That's understandable.'

'Yes?'

'Of course.' I pat her hand where it is still lying across my thigh. Warm, long fingers.

'But he does not need to be concerned.'

'How do you mean?'

Consuela lifts her hand away, presses her palms together, rubs her right temple as though there is a stab of pain. 'Because you will not leave me, Jim. Because you love me, don't you?'

'Of course.'

'You are not going away, Jim?' She rubs at her temple again, bites her lip and I think there is a trace of tear in the corner of her eye.

'Of course not. Don't you worry about Ernesto, he's just anxious about his little sister.'

I miss the gear on the corner I've slowed down for, the gears crunch, the sound of pain and complaint. I jab them into place, pick up speed, eyes on the road.

Almost a year later I have my suitcase packed again, but it's not a trip this time. Today I'll leave her.

'Are you well, Jim?' Consuela runs a hand over my forehead and stands back.

'I'm fine.'

'You don't want your breakfast?'

'I'm just not very hungry this morning.'

'But you will drink your tea?'

I stand up too abruptly, catch the flash of hurt in her eyes.

'I've just got a bit of a headache. Come here.'

I pull her to me to me, hold her close, stroke her long, silky hair, take in her scent: warm, clean skin fresh from the shower, the slight tang of limey kalamansi, the suggestion of coconut from the shampoo she uses, smells I will always remember. She turns her face up after a moment and kisses me. She tastes of the mango she has just eaten for breakfast. I hold her at arm's length.

'Let me look at you.' She has a way of blushing, a tiny hint of colour behind the soft brown evenness of her young skin. She is wearing a white silk robe that comes to her knees, a trail of flowers, lime green stems and floppy headed pink blooms run down the front, following the contour of her body. Her stomach is flat, the way only a stomach that has never been stretched by pregnancy can be flat. I press the flat of my palm onto her stomach and she smiles, bites her lower lip, then grins.

'You are pleased, Jim?'

'Yes.' I let my fingers move away slowly, blink hard and make for the bathroom where I can take deep breaths. I slide down the wall and sit hunched up with my head in my hands for a minute.

Consuela is sitting at the table when I emerge, humming between sips of tea.

'I'd better be off then. Are you going to the market today?'

'Yes, Jim. Is there anything special that you want?'

'No, Cariad, you just take care of yourself.'

Consuela moves her hand to her flat stomach that is protecting my son and smiles. 'I will, Jim.'

She stands to kiss me. 'Bye, Jim, have a good day.'

'And you, Cariad, and you. You take really good care now.'

She nods effusively, waves from the window as I drive the car out of the gate, held open by a guard wearing the uniform of the American firm I work for – worked for, I correct myself.

I drive a little way through the estate. The taxi will pick Consuela up soon. Punctuality is not a virtue here, but it will be early, it comes every Tuesday and Consuela likes to get to the market before the produce begins to wilt in the heat and humidity.

When I go back into the house I have a sudden wish for a camera. If I only had pictures: of this house, of the trip to Baguio, most of all of Consuela. But I can't take pictures home. If Cath were to find them... I shake myself into focus, walk past the door of the front small bedroom that Consuela has made her sewing room, full of bright scraps and emerging patchwork quilts. I open our bedroom door.

For a moment I take it all in. The walls are pale terracotta. The floor is hardwood, not dark, not light, polished and clean. On the bed is the blue quilt that Consuela bought while we were still living in the hotel and across the quilt Consuela has left her white silk robe. I reach under the bed and pull out my grey suitcase, edged with a thin red stripe. I open it and take the passport from the top, flick it open to check it and tuck it into the inside pocket of my light navy jacket. It crosses my mind to tuck the white silk robe into the top of the suitcase, but it will only cause trouble when Cath finds it. Instead I lift up the silk, breathe it in and let it fall back onto the bed. I run my hand over it, smooth and cool, soft as young skin.

Before I close the case I pull out the fat cream envelope, flick it open. The note, the money: all in place. I leave it on the dark rattan bedside table, zip the case rapidly and take it all in again. My eye catches on the bulging envelope by the bed. I scoop it up, walk out of the bedroom with my case and the envelope, two steps down the corridor. I look around the kitchen, its cleanness, its whiteness, the smells of hygiene and fruit. I walk to the far end of the room where the little round white table stands beside the patio doors, west facing for the best view of the sunsets and cooler in the mornings. I put the envelope on the table and turn to leave, but wonder again if this is the best place for the envelope. I don't want to leave the money by the bed, it might seem like... But she might need to lie down and miss it on the table. I hurry back to the bedroom and put the envelope on the bed, on Consuela's white silk robe.

I want to walk round the whole house again, one last time, make sure I have the pictures in my head, but I have to be at Nikoy Aquino by nine and the morning traffic is always bad. I take a deep breath; turn right out of the kitchen, along the little passage past our bedroom, Consuela's sewing room, through the solid hardwood front door and out. I pull the door closed, unhook the house keys from my keychain and post them into the letterbox.

'Are you alright there, Mr Vaughan?'

'Fine thanks, Julio.' I move the case carefully round the car so that the guard won't see it. 'Had to come back for some paperwork.'

He nods. 'You have a nice day, Mr Vaughan.'

'Thanks, Julio.' I wonder if I should say something about looking after Consuela, give him some extra money. 'You have a nice day as well.'

Nikoy Aquino is just any other airport on the planet, big and loud, full of frazzled people stumbling from one place to the next with stunned looks on their faces. My plane, a Cathay Pacific Boeing 747, is on time. I rush on board. Consuela might have the letter by now, might be opening and reading it right now, the fat wodge of money spilling on the white robe. But better than the bedside table. It's just over two hours to Chek Lap Kok airport in Hong Kong, where I have to start all over again: customs, boarding, a 777 jet this time for the long haul, thirteen hours.

When we land at Heathrow terminal three, the flight crew announce that it's nine o'clock in the evening, British Summer Time – five past nine to be precise. My thick gold watch says four o'clock, four in the morning for Consuela. Is she asleep? Is she sitting at the little white table sipping tea and crying? What have I done? What else could I do?

'I suppose you're thinking about her, are you? Your black tart, I mean.'

'Let's just give it a rest, Cath.'

'Give it a rest? I haven't started yet,' Cath hisses. But
she falls silent again.

Going Home

Megan says carefully, 'I thought I should make a start on dinner.'

Jim and Cath stare at her, as though neither of them know who she is for a moment. Cath is hunched on the sofa. Her eyes look puffy, Megan thinks. Jim is perched uneasily on the armchair, as though he might need to bolt at any moment.

'I could do some chicken pieces, maybe, with some new potatoes and salad?'

Jim blinks. 'That would be nice, Cariad.'

'Are we staying?' Cath asks abruptly.

'Pardon?' Jim unfolds out of the chair and stretches. 'Sounds alright doesn't it? A bit of chicken?'

'I'm not talking about the chicken. I just thought we should be going.'

'Bit of a long drive at this time of night, Love, don't you think?' Jim glances at his watch: almost five-thirty.

Cath jabs at the air towards Jim. 'Did she give you that gold watch? Your fancy bit?'

Jim lowers his arm so that the watch tucks itself under his shirt sleeve, walks towards the living room window so that his back is turned on Cath. 'The rain's stopped, I see.'

'Where did you get that watch?'

'It'd take us a good six hours, you know, maybe a bit longer, but if you want to get going...'

'Shit!' Cath stands, stalks across the living room and pushes past Jim. She slams the living room door on her way upstairs to the bathroom, so that the whole house shakes.

'Think your mam wants to get going, Megan,' Jim says. 'Probably best just to do something for you and Ben.'

This is how it will be: the drive home, the silence broken only by the occasional hiss of an insult or some half articulated fury from Cath. Jim will nod slightly, in a way that is new, a movement he has picked up that might mean yes or no, and which will infuriate Cath further. Jim will concentrate hard on the road, so hard that Cath's words race past him with the blur of white lines that mark the road: whore, tart, pig, cow. He will drive faster.

'Bloody listen to what I'm saying, you pig.'

Jim fancies a pig farm, a dream that stops at some indeterminate time of resignation. He's not so bothered about cows, but a horse, now a horse or two would be...

'Are you listening to a word I'm saying?'

No one listens to her, but she had to listen. *'Cath Parry, what did I say?' Palms down on the desk. The crack of pain.*

Jim will keep his eyes on the road, put his foot down. Words will only add to the confusion.

'You will listen to me. I'll make you bloody listen.'

'Write a hundred times: I must pay attention in class. Do you hear?' The last biting rap of the ruler cuts across her knuckles.

She has to listen to everyone, but no-one will listen to her. Next to her Jim will drive, eyes averted from her, impassive. Cath will flare in another wave of invective. She will explode if he doesn't rise to the bait, if he doesn't make some answer. She will make him live from one punishment to the next. At home she will throw things at him, scream at him. Sometimes hurling insults or furniture will not be enough.

'Jim! You're still not listening. Listen! Say something!'

There will be silence except for the small whir of the engine, speed rising. Cath will put her head to the window so that the vibration jolts and jars her body. She will take comfort in the discomfort, press harder, let fat tears slide down her red, angry face from her sunken, dark-ringed green eyes, sniff noisily.

Jim will settle at eighty miles an hour, eyes resolutely forward, so fixed he can hardly see anything at all. He will clutch the steering wheel so that the tightness of his grip, not the motion of the car, leaves a persistent aching judder along his arms, jaw clenched, shoulders knotted in tension.

Cath's head will ache. She will feel how the press of the window sets her whole skull on edge, how exhausted and dehydrated she is from the useless tears that will not turn Jim's eyes from the road for a moment.

'You used to think a lot of me.'

'Yes.'

'What's that supposed to mean?'

'Nothing.'

'What do you mean?'

Jim will sigh and shrug.

'What the hell's that supposed to be?'

'Nothing.'

'Bastard! Did you treat your fancy black tart like this? Is that why she got rid of you?'

Silence.

'I asked you a question.'

Silence.

'Don't think I won't make your life hell when we get home. I'll give you such bloody hell, I'll... You'll wish you'd never been born.'

'I suppose so.'

Cath will let out a scream so piercing that Jim nearly lets go of the steering wheel. He will clutch harder as she thumps the dashboard with both fists.

'Megan has no idea what you're really like, does she? Tada's little girl with her "let's talk reasonably" and "let's be constructive". I told her, the only reason I'm taking you back is to get my revenge. It's on my terms now, Jim, so you'd better watch yourself if you don't want to wake up with a knife in your guts.'

'No.'

'What?'

'I wouldn't wake up, would I?'

'What?'

'If I had a knife in my guts I wouldn't wake up.'

'Will you talk some bloody sense for a change? If you can't talk sense you'd better shut your mouth.'

'Yes'

The scream of frustration will burst against Jim's eardrum again, the car will swerve slightly, be pulled back into line. He will frown as the dashboard of the hire car takes another blow, but hold his peace, eyes forwards.

Silence.

'Don't know what the silly cow saw in you, anyway.' This time Cath mumbles, petulant, tired. 'Must've been desperate, the dirty whore you shacked up with. How old did you say she was?'

'Fancy a cup of tea?'

'What?'

'We're coming up to a service station.'

'So?'

'Thought you might be ready for a drink.'

Cath will feel the parched ache in her mouth, the steady thump of a pulse in her aching head. 'Stuff your bloody tea.'

'Maybe a bite to eat?'

'Are you bloody *listening* to me? I said stuff your bloody drink and your bite to eat.'

'Ah.'

'What you doing?' Cath will twist awkwardly in her seat towards the receding slip road.

'What?'

'I thought you were stopping at that service station?'

'But you said...'

'Like you give a toss what I say.'

'But...'

'Shut your face!' Cath will shout so that the air in the car reverberates.

She will begin to cry, noisily this time, as Jim speeds up. She will hold a hand to her temple, feel sick with the headache. But with more than seven hours since she last ate, even she will not be able to will herself to vomit in the car that Jim has hired and will have to account for.

'Swine,' she will mutter, but he will not answer back.

This is how it will be: the useless wrangles, the long streams of curses and interrogation with no answers, only evasion, the blank harshness of closed doors, the frustration that will drive her to new feats of torment.

'I cut all the sleeves off those bloody silk shirts today.'

'What?'

'You heard.'

159

Cath will dip her head back into the magazine that she is not reading, her red hair faded to a dull brown that melds with the Draylon brown of the sofa.

'What's that in aid of?' Jim will run a weary hand through dark hair that is greasy.

'I don't want foreign muck in this house.'

Jim will sit down heavily on a frail dining chair that creaks under his weight, at the other end of the long open plan room in the house that Cath chose. Behind the fruit bowl will be a pile of meticulously cut paper, cream and almost maroon red, a film of photo paper.

'What's this?' Jim will sift through the shreds, his head shaking slowly.

'What does it look like?'

'You can't just...'

'What do you mean I can't? I have, haven't I? Anyway you won't be needing it again, you're not going anywhere, are you?'

'Cath, you can't just cut up passports.'

'Well I have.'

Jim will lift both hands to his head, rest a moment and stand. 'I'm going to put the kettle on. Want some tea?'

'What time is it?'

'About five, I think, my watch's upstairs.'

'Is it?'

'Is what?'

'Your watch.'

'Cath?'

Jim will cross to the door, resist slamming it behind him, bound upstairs. The gold watch will be on the bedside table in his single bedded room, where he left it; the face ground into a mess of fine glass and metal fragments. Jim will sit on the bed, head in his hands, cradling himself, rocking slightly.

Then a flash of panic as he scrambles under the bed, lifts the carpet in the far corner, the corner hidden from even Cath's hoovering: the ring, its gold plaits beaten into a single curve, will be there still, hidden, the only thing left.

'I'll make that cup of tea then,' Jim will say flatly, back downstairs.

'You do that,' Cath says, head back in the glossy magazine, pretending to read an article: *Fifty Ways to Keep Your Lover.*

The job as a postman will be much harder than Jim expects: getting the round done in time. He will come home in the afternoon tired, trail upstairs to change out of the uniform. He will take a deep breath before he opens the back bedroom door, steady himself. One day the drawers will be emptied onto the floor, the wardrobe doors will be open, clothes strewn across the room. Nothing broken, only some folding and tidying; not a bad day. He will shuffle into the bathroom, turn on the shower. Downstairs Cath will be cooking, so that he can smell the tastes he missed in Manila: lamb chops perhaps, overcooked, but welcome.

He will walk into the room carefully, no missiles. A good day perhaps.

'Dinner's nearly ready, sweetheart,' Cath will call through from the kitchen off the long open plan front room.

Jim will wince, sit down gingerly at the dining room table with its thin legged chairs that creak.

Cath will bring in the plate, her hand protected from its heat by a tea towel, white with blue stripes, the kind that children use for shepherd costumes in school nativity plays.

Jim will manage a thin smile. 'Smells good, Love.'

'Glad you think so.'

Jim will close his eyes, brace himself.

Cath will stand at his side, square up to the table, lift the plate higher and let it drop so that it makes a dull thud against the scratched surface of the wood, the shards of ceramic spattering amongst soggy peas and carrots.

'Maybe I'll just have a bacon butty,' Jim will say, his voice too even.

He will wait until Cath has stormed upstairs, crying and shouting, before he clears away the wrecked dinner. He will eat the sandwich standing in the kitchen, chewing fast between mouthfuls of strong, bitter tea. Cath will be back in the living room, stock still on the sofa, eyes dried, feet tucked under her, an ordinary middle aged woman reading a magazine: *How to Keep the Excitement in your Marriage.*

Jim will sit down in the big arm chair, flick the TV remote: nothing.

'Must be out of batteries,' Jim will comment to the air.

'If you like.'

'What?'

Jim will walk over to the side board, a long cupboard that matches the dining set, a leftover from the first house in Blaenau, rummage in the top drawer for batteries. From the arm chair, Jim will flick the remote again: nothing.

'Think this remote's on the blink, Cath.'

'If you say so.'

Jim will stand up, take a step, lean over and jab at the TV 'on' button: nothing. 'Maybe something's up with the telly.'

'You think?'

'Has it been on today?'

'What?'

'The telly. Was it working earlier?'

'It was working last time I used it.' Cath will press her face further towards the magazine, but not before Jim notices a thin, smug smile.

Jim will pull the heavy oak TV cabinet forward a little, peer round the back. 'Bloody hell, Cath.'

'What?' She will look up, defiant, grinning.

'There's no need for that.'

'What?'

'You've cut the plug off the telly.'

'Didn't I mention it?'

'Bloody hell.' Jim will slump into the chair, the prospect of an evening of silence or sniping ahead. 'What the hell's wrong with you?'

'Me? What's wrong with me? You've got a bloody nerve, asking what's wrong with me. I'm not the one gallivanting round the world with little black tarts. There's nothing wrong with me.'

'There's no need for all this, Cath.'

'So you keep saying.' Cath will hurl the magazine across the room, head for the shelf above the fire. Jim will be half way through the living room door before the paper weight hits it and explodes, glass and liquid spewing down the door.

In his bedroom there will be no plug on the radio clock. He will slide onto the bed, pick up his racing form book and flick through: every second page missing, scored down the margin and ripped out to leave jagged strips. He will pick up yesterday's paper, sigh and begin to read.

This is how it will be: he will not talk, he will not let her have Consuela, but he will break.

One day Cath will stand still, her hand still raised with the blue and white tea towel in it. She will freeze. On the table will be another smashed plate, another wasted dinner, but something new will happen. When the roaring noise stops, Jim will throw back his chair, one frail leg finally snapping as the chair lands awkwardly. He will walk across the room, wrench the blank, plug-less television from the dark oak mock Georgian cabinet, splintering one of the doors as he tugs the TV free to hurl it across the living room towards the open plan dining area where Cath will still be standing, motionless.

'I've had enough. Do you hear?'

Cath will find her voice again, a thin, shaken hiss, but defiant.

'I haven't even started yet.' She will walk into the kitchen, shut the door behind her and sink down with her back to the door. The shaking won't stop, but she will smile, feel a rush of adrenalin.

There will be an odd, sour joy in finding this shared, perverse delight, a companionship. For a few minutes, or even half-an-hour during the most satisfying frenzies, they will annihilate the contents of their home, compete to better one another in acts of destruction that bring fleeting relief. They will begin to long for the next adrenalin rush. The house will lie in ruins: sofa and chair slashed and oozing foam padding, curtains ripped, no ornaments left. Unwary feet might pick up the last remains of the small treasures that were given as Christmas presents by Megan and Elin when they were small: the shard of an orange pot that Megan brought home from a school trip, a fragment from a blue glass dolphin that Elin found in jumble sale when she was ten, splinters of wood from a shattered drawer out of a chest given to Cath and Jim by Sarah not long before she died, the debris left at the foot of the stairs.

One day Jim will slam out of the front door. 'I'll be at the pub, might get some food for a change.'

'Just don't pick up any black whores,' Cath will scream after him. 'You never know what else you might pick up from them.'

She will sit on the torn red-brown sofa for a while, feel the rush subside. She will get up and pace, go into the kitchen, find a bottle of whisky at the back of the cupboard under the sink, hidden behind weed-killer and bleach.

This is how it will be. But today, Monday July 16th 1990, this life is ahead of them. Jim drives along the motorway, face set to the road, the summer light dulled by clouds, his wife at his side, tense, red-eyed, sniffing back tears and hissing insults heading for home.

'Tell me about your home, Jim.'
'What about it?'
'What colour is it?'
'Grey. Grey slate. Grey houses. Grey Grey rain. Grey people when I think about it.'

In the night-time rain two men cling to each other outside a hastily-erected army tent.

'I have to get back, I promised I would help some more.'

'No-one will expect you,' Rodriguez tells his father. 'You should go home, you need sleep.'

'How can I sleep, Rodriguez?' Antonio returns.

'I know, I know. But you must rest at least.'

'How can we lose so many?' Antonio holds his hands to his head, as though it might otherwise explode.

'I don't know.'

Rodriguez feels his tears well again. They have not brought out Ernesto's body yet. His brother is still in the factory, but they know that he is dead, trapped in the burned out shell of the building. The district where Ernesto lives, *lived* – Rodriguez reminds himself, is beyond a road that has become a fissure in the earth, a deep rift. Leonora, Ernesto's wife, their four children will not have heard yet. That is still to be faced, but they have the others. His mother, Isabella, the life crushed out of her, but recognisable, and his baby sister, are inside the tent set up outside the hospital in case the aftershocks should bring down the building. There is no news of his younger brother, Antonio, working out in the mountains at the art centre where the tourists come to buy carvings and quilts, baskets and wall hangings. There is no news of Juanita, the girl who has Ernesto's fifth child, fatherless now. Ernesto was only with her for two years, not long enough for recognition.

'Consuela has never had good luck,' Rodriguez says quietly, as much to himself as to his father.

Antonio shakes his head, but even now there is a nod, assent and denial in one. 'But this?'

Antonio raises his hands to heaven and begins to weep again. Rodriguez clings to his father and they stand in the rain, crying.

The Way Things Are

Elin drives back through the City, across Waterloo bridge, down the Strand, through the slow crawl of snarled up traffic around Harrods, heading west, then north. She has promised Terry that she will begin looking over the last quarter's accounts for his business, but she can't think about that.

She pulls up outside her Victorian terraced house. The house prices locally are rocketing and Terry wants to sell now that he has finished the renovations, but Elin will not move; they will never need anywhere bigger. Elin twists the key in the stiff lock of the red door, pushes into the hallway: original black and terracotta tiles on the floor, original cornice work and dado rail highlighted in white, bordering the freshly painted panels of Georgian blue and turquoise that run along the passage and up the stairs. She walks past the two small living rooms and into the orange kitchen, screws her eyes up against the brightness for a moment. In the pine corner cupboard are more bright colours, mugs in cobalt blue and sunshine orange.

She reaches instead for a glass and runs the tap, splashes the cool water on her face and fills the glass. Upstairs, in the mercifully pale bathroom – eau-de-nil Terry calls it – Elin runs a bath. She reaches for a bottle of paracetamol and takes two pills with the glass of water. She leaves the bottle on the side of the bath while she goes to fetch what she needs. In the hot, foam-filled water Elin leans back and sighs deeply. It is eleven o'clock. Terry won't be home until six at least. She has seven hours, more time than she needs.

'Look, Megan, look!' Elin waves a headless baby doll in the air and rolls on the carpet, giggling.

'Elin! Your babies. They're your babies.'

Elin sits up and looks into her sister's serious green eyes, her own eyes flashing with green mischief. 'They're only dolls,' Elin says emphatically.

'Yes, but they're all broken now. What did you do that for? Where's Mam?'

'In the garden.'

Megan peers out of the back window, to where her mother is struggling against the wind with white sheets.

'Well, don't let Mam see these. Let's take them up to your room.'

'Tada's in my room having a rest. Why is Tada always in my room?'

'So you can sleep with Mam.'

'Why do I have to sleep with Mam?'

'Because of your nightmares, because you have bad dreams, Elin. Mam can look after you if you wake up.'

'I don't have bad dreams. I don't wake up.'

'Well maybe you cry in your sleep, maybe you have bad dreams that you don't remember in the morning.'

Megan scoops up the dolls and ducks into the hallway as Cath comes through the back door.

'Are you playing nice, Elin?' Megan hears Cath call from the kitchen as she heads upstairs with an armful of Elin's headless dolls.

'Megan took all my dolls away.' Elin begins to giggle again and roll on the floor.

'What?' Cath puts a weary head into the room. 'I'm too busy to be sorting out your squabbles.'

Elin sits up on the carpet, her red hair is tangled and there is a stain on her dress, Cath notices with annoyance.

'Well Megan can take you in the garden and push you on the swing. Where is she?'

Elin splashes the foam around her, leans forward to top up the hot water, unfastens the lid on the bottle and leans back, sinking into the warm bergamot-scented bubbles. Her hand strays onto her flat tummy. She will be twenty-five tomorrow.

Would be twenty-five, she corrects herself.

Elin remembers creeping out of bed, away from the sour smell of her sleeping mother. She is ten years old and she no longer believes in the stories of her nightmares, but she is still stuck here with Mam, night after night, while Megan gets her own bedroom and her dad sleeps in the room that should be hers. Not fair, Elin tells herself as usual. She creeps across the landing and leans on the handle of the bathroom door, but it's locked.

'Megan? Megan is that you?' Elin whispers, glancing back at the bedroom where her mother is snoring loudly. 'I need the toilet, Megan,' Elin hisses, trying to sound urgent and stay quiet.

If she wakes up Mam, Megan will be in trouble. Everything is Megan's fault. Elin knows this, but it brings her no comfort. She doesn't want Mam shouting at Megan, she just wants her own room back.

From behind the bathroom door Elin hears a noise like something not human, a chilling low note that makes her shiver, her stomach clenching in knots. She thinks she might wet herself if she doesn't get to the toilet soon, or if she hears that noise again.

'Megan, are you sick? Shall I get Mam?'

'No!' Megan's voice sounds strange, but she hears the bolt slide and the door opens an inch. Elin catches a glimmer of her sister in the dark, her skin looks pale and clammy, but Megan pulls back quickly, crouching behind the door. 'There's no need to get Mam, Elin, it's nothing.' Elin has the impression that Megan has to concentrate hard on every word. 'Just fetch me some old towels.'

Elin slips open the airing cupboard on the landing and grabs a handful of towels, then remembers that Megan said to bring old ones. She discards the good towels on the floor and scrambles back to the door.

Megan's hands are already raised around the door frame, waiting for the towels and she pulls them out of Elin's hands, but she does say thank you, Elin notices with satisfaction.

The urge to get to the toilet is even stronger now, heightened by an odd feeling of her own importance.

'Can I pee?' Elin says, crossing her legs and moving urgently from side to side.

Megan opens the door a crack further.

'You'll have to hurry up, Elin.'

As Elin slides through the barely open door she notices Megan tucking towels around herself. Megan looks shiny and sick and she stays huddled against the bath instead of leaving the room while Elin uses the toilet. Elin looks away and hunches onto the toilet bowl without even lowering the seat. The coldness of the porcelain shoots through her. She can see Megan watching her, the way her best friend's dog looks when it has stolen a piece of chicken. She tries not to look back.

'I'm fine, Elin. It's just...'

'Is it your period?'

'Yes.'

Elin stands up and thinks better of flushing the chain, in case Mam wakes. She wants to stay with Megan or she doesn't want to leave Megan, who looks more green and ill with each second.

'God, I never want periods!' Elin thinks how lame that sounds. She watches Megan shut her eyes and bite into her lip as she scrunches over in pain.

'You'd better go now, Elin. Go back to bed quietly. Don't wake Mam.'

Elin nods and backs out of the bathroom. In bed she thinks she can hear that noise again, she wonders if someone can die from a period. If Megan dies it will be her fault for doing nothing. She prods her mother, who turns and snorts and settles into a new pattern of snoring. Elin prods harder.

'Mam, Mam! Wake up Mam. Megan's ill. Megan's in the bathroom, Mam. I think she's dying. Wake up, Mam.'

Elin strokes her flat tummy again. 'No baby,' she says out loud. She thinks of the baby Megan is carrying now, Ben's baby, and starts to cry softly.

Elin is thirteen when Megan leaves home. In the August after Elin's thirteenth birthday, a damp, grey day when nothing much special happens, Megan takes Elin with her to collect the results of her A-levels. Megan's friends are all talking too loud, full of bravado while they wait in line for their envelopes.

When Megan opens her envelope, Elin is swept along by the nervous hysteria of the place and grabs Megan's card before Megan can see for herself what the grades are. Elin squeals and does a little dance, hopping from foot to foot.

'Oh, my God, Megan. All 'A'. You got 'A's for everything: English: 'A', French: 'A', General Studies: 'A', Philosophy: 'A', English Special Paper: Grade 1.'

Megan grins and hugs her. Later, when they've been to Ginetto's ice cream parlour with a bunch of Megan's friends, they go home and tell Mam about Megan getting an 'A' for everything, but Mam doesn't say anything. She puckers her face and mutters something mean under her breath. There's no point in doing anything good, Elin thinks.

After that, the tension at breakfast time is worse every day. Mam hates Ben. A week later Megan is gone and Elin knows she's on her own. There's no point doing anything, being good at anything or making friends.

Most mornings Elin feels sick before she goes to school. She can't listen to anything in class, not that she was ever the shiny favourite of the teachers like Megan. The bullies sniff out Elin's weary resignation and circle her with jibes or worse. Some mornings her stomach knots against her. She can't make herself get ready for school and Mam doesn't make her go.

'Can't see the point in all this bloody exam palaver,' Mam says. 'It's not like you'll amount to anything.'

The bath water has begun to cool slightly and Elin leans towards the authentic Victorian tap to let more heat run into the scented water.

*

'I said get out of bloody bed!' Cath is red in the face.

'Why?' Elin clings to the bed cover, slides back down under it.

'It's your birthday. You should get up.'

'Why?' Elin says listlessly from under the cover.

'I've got you a present. Come and see what I've got you.' Cath coaxes half heartedly. There is no reply. 'You can't stay in bloody bed forever.'

'You did.'

'What? What are you talking about? When do I stay in bed?'

'When I was little.'

'I don't know what you're talking about Elin, now get up.' Cath tugs at the blanket, a fierce, aggressive tug, but Elin has a firm grip. 'For God's sake, Elin, this room bloody stinks. You haven't had a bath in I don't know how long. Get up and come and open your bloody present!'

'Don't want to,' Elin says, a flat small voice from under the cover.

'I give up! I bloody give up! Rot away in here if that's what you want. I'll have the bloody school on my back next and then where will we be? You've already had warnings. It will be Social Services after me next. Still, what do you care about anyone but yourself, you're getting just like your sister.'

'I want Megan to come home.'

'What?'

Elin peers over the cover, grey faced, her green eyes sunken.

'What a bloody mess you look. No-one would believe you're a young girl. What the hell have you got

173

to be depressed about? You're fifteen, you don't know you're bloody born yet.'

'I want to see Megan.'

'Well you can't.' Cath seizes her moment to make another lunge for the cover, leaving Elin huddled against the head board on a rumpled sheet.

'Why?' Elin is tearful now.

'Because she ran off with that bastard-English boyfriend of hers and I won't have her in my house.'

'He's not her boyfriend. They've been married for two years nearly.'

Elin curls into a ball, tight as a fist and begins to sob.

'Are you getting up today or what?' Cath says, panting as she shakes the cover off the duvet to take it to the wash.

Elin goes on sobbing, squeezing herself tighter and tighter into a closed ball.

'Well, do what you like, everyone always does.'

Cath bangs downstairs, slams the kitchen door behind her so that above, Elin's bed shakes with the vibration. Cath turns on the radio, louder and louder until Elin can hardly hear her own sobbing.

The water is cooling again, and there might not be much hot water left, Elin thinks, even in the oversized tank that Terry has installed. She tugs at the plug, listens as the water is sucked out, pushes the plug back in and turns on the hot tap again. She wonders briefly about writing a note, but what would she say? That she hasn't laughed since the last time she pulled the head off a baby doll?

Elin leans forward and takes hold of the bottle. She unscrews the safety lid and begins eating the pills.

'Pain-killers,' she says to the empty room.

The tablets are harder to swallow than she had imagined. She reaches out of the bath towards the little table that is cluttered with brushes, combs, hair slides, a necklace Terry gave her for her last birthday. She picks the glass up from the tangle of objects and fills it from the bath tap. With the water to help her, Elin keeps working through the tablets. When the bottle is empty, she reaches for the blister pack of Prozac, each blister labelled with a day of the week like novelty knickers or the contraceptives that have become an irrelevance.

She feels bloated from gulping the water down constantly and nauseous, but it may be only the anticipation, she thinks. Surely the pills can't be working yet. She has to act carefully. She read somewhere that it must be both wrists. She doesn't know if it's true, but she wants to take no chances. Elin holds the knife carefully in her right hand. She hopes that her left hand, the hand she favours, will be strong enough still to do the job after the left hand vein has been cut. If she avoids the artery on the left side the blood will still be pumping. Where did she hear that? She knows that the cut has to be hard. She has already experimented higher on her right arm. It takes much more pressure than she had imagined, not at all like cutting through butter, even butter cold from the fridge. But she knows it will work. The cuts on her upper arm sting in the bath water. Is it true that it is painless?

Elin leans forward and slices deep across the veins of her left wrist. The sting makes her catch her breath and she pushes her hand into the water, gingerly lifts it out a little way. Good, the blood is dark, no arteries hit on this side. She clasps the knife in her injured left hand, braces herself for the moment of pain, just a moment she tells herself, and slashes across the right wrist, further out this time to take in the artery.

The crimson blood spurts more than a foot into the air, pulses steadily. Elin leans back into the slow spread of viscous red bubbles, closes her eyes, sinks further into the bath and waits.

The End of the Day

Megan hugs Ben tightly.

'You have no idea how pleased I am to see you.'

'Well, there's a welcome. Good day?' Ben grins, holding Megan at arms' length.

'The best,' Megan says. 'I've got some chicken on, it'll be ready in ten minutes. Do you want some wine?'

'That'd be lovely. Was it very awful?'

Ben follows Megan into the tiny kitchen, winds his arms around her waist, leaning his head on her shoulder as she reaches into the cupboard for a wine glass.

'Yes. Yes, I think it was. They don't exactly talk.'

Megan twists to peck Ben on the cheek and ducks out from under his arms.

'How was Elin?' Ben asks.

Megan pours wine into Ben's glass from the open bottle she has retrieved from the fridge, pours orange juice into her tumbler.

'She looked ill, but she wouldn't come in. I don't know whether she just wanted to be rid of Mam at the earliest possible moment, which is pretty understandable, or whether she couldn't bear to see Dad. I think the baby makes her feel uncomfortable as well. I'm sure she regrets the sterilisation, but she won't talk about it. I ache for her Ben, she always looks so ill, she always has headaches and all she gets from the doctor is more anti-depressants. Last time I saw her properly she said a really odd thing. We were talking about Dad disappearing to the Philippines, not thinking he'd come home of course, and she said, "Now you know what it feels like when he abandons you". When Elin was born I told my dad that Mam could have the baby and he could keep me. I was only five, but that's how it always was and you always think you're the one who got the worst deal, but I don't really know. It's like we had these separate childhoods.'

Ben listens, sipping wine and nodding. 'They're quite an act, aren't they, your family?'

'You could say. Elin said she'd ring later. Come and sit down with me while we wait for dinner. I want a long bath and a good film to watch tonight.'

Ben sits close to Megan on the sofa. 'Not something weepy; please not *Truly, Madly, Deeply*.' Ben ducks from Megan's mock punches then pulls her close to him.

'No, not tonight, something very light. *Moonstruck*?'

'I could live with that. "Won't somebody tell a joke?"' Ben parodies in a fake Italian American accent.

'Precisely.'

The phone rings. 'That's probably Elin. Will you have a look at the chicken for me?'

'Will do. I'll set the table while I'm up.'

'Terry, slow down, I'm sorry, I don't understand... What do you mean? But how? I mean... I...'

Megan stands by the phone in the alcove under the stairs holding onto the receiver, the line dead, gazing at nothing.

'Megan, are you alright, Love? You look pale. God Megan, what's wrong?'

'Elin,' Megan says, almost inaudibly.

Ben dislodges the receiver from Megan's clenched fist, listens to check that no-one is still on the line and hangs up the phone. He steers Megan back towards the sofa and makes her sit.

'Is something wrong with Elin, Megan?' Ben bends over her solicitously.

Megan gasps out a dry, choked sob. 'She...she... Terry found her in the bath.'

Ben has had to lean in closer to hear what Megan is saying. He starts back. 'Found her? Has she done something?'

Megan nods, then begins to weep fat, hot tears that fill her up. She gulps out occasional words through the crying. 'We have...to go... Terry is...on his own.'

'Is Elin...is she alive?'

Megan shakes her head, pulls herself into a tight ball on the sofa, rocks and wails loudly.

'My God. Okay, let's go, if you're sure, I mean if that's what you want. I'll just turn off the oven. What about your parents?'

'They won't be home for hours, there's no way to get in touch with them till they're home.'

'Okay, well that'll have to wait, then. Oh Megan, I'm so sorry, love, I'm so, so sorry.' Ben holds Megan, stroking her long red hair as she cries and rocks.

'Is it really only half past ten? Mam and Dad won't even be back home yet. I told Terry I'd ring them.' Megan says when they arrive home four hours after the phone call.

'You should go to bed,' Ben replies.

'I won't be able to sleep.' Megan subsides onto the sofa.

'I'll wait up and ring your parents later. They probably won't be there until about midnight, Megan. You look exhausted.'

Megan smiles weakly, raises herself a little. 'I ache all over.'

Ben sits next to her and strokes her hair. 'How about...no, sorry, maybe not such a good idea.'

'What?' Megan twists to look into Ben's face. 'You can say "bath", Ben.'

He smiles weakly. 'Sorry, of course. Would you like a bath?'

'Not yet. Just hold me.'

'Of course. Are you hungry?'

Megan laughs lightly. 'I'm starving. It seems so horrible to feel something as mundane as hunger when my sister is dead doesn't it? Am I horrible?'

'No, love, you're not horrible, you're just...' Ben hesitates. 'You're just alive, Megan. I'll get you some of the chicken.' He gets up and goes to the kitchen.

'She's been unhappy since she went to school, maybe before that, but when she found Terry... I thought...'

Ben puts his head round the opening to the kitchen. 'But they lived with your mother at the beginning and then your mum pretty much moved in with them when your dad went AWOL. They didn't get much of a chance, did they? A couple of years in the middle and even then your mum was always back and forth to stay with them.' Ben pauses. 'Maybe Terry wanted children.'

'I know, but it's so...'

'Final, Megan. I think that was the point. She'd had enough. Here, try and eat something.'

Megan surveys the chicken and salad, pushes it around the plate, nibbles at fragments. 'I've lost my appetite. Maybe she wouldn't have felt like she'd had enough if we'd helped more.'

'Don't go there. "Ifs" don't really exist. You'll only torture yourself for nothing.'

'I know.'

'Let me run you a bath. There's nearly another hour before we can ring your parents.'

'Okay.' Megan pushes wearily out of the enveloping sofa and follows Ben upstairs.

In the bathroom Megan watches Ben tip half a bottle of lavender bubbles into the steaming water, swirl the bubbles under the taps so that they foam and froth. He lays out a big towel on the stool beside the bath, a blue so pale it is almost white.

Megan forces herself to the bedroom, sits on the bed for a moment, pulls off her shoes, lets the cotton print skirt fall on the floor. She pulls the white t-shirt over her head, pulls down the straps of her lacy white bra and swivels the fastener to the front to unhook. She slides her white cotton knickers down, stands and stretches. She turns to the long bedroom mirror and runs a hand over her body that still hardly reveals the pregnancy. She looks more closely at herself: her green eyes are tear stained, her long red hair needs combing, her breasts feel heavier recently, but not yet sagged, the curve of her stomach that will soon swell. Megan turns and reaches for the cobalt blue towelling bathrobe and savours the thickness of the material, the softness of the velveteen. She walks slowly to the bathroom, a few steps across the landing, and stands beside Ben. She reaches up and puts her arms around him, holding on tightly, eyes closed as she lifts her face and kisses him, a long slow kiss. When she opens her eyes Ben eases her bathrobe from her and helps her into the hot, scented water. He smiles and leaves Megan to settle into the soothing foam.

After You'd Gone

In the delivery room the lights are as piercing as an interrogation.

She lies on her side slightly, feels the momentary sharp jab of the spinal needle.

'Tell me when you can't feel any pain here.'

The doctor works through careful stages, follows the growing numbness inch by inch up Megan's body.

'Okay, that seems to be fine. We're just going to put this screen across here to shield you from the messy bits. You probably don't want to actually see the knife.' The young obstetrician grins. Megan nods. She feels heavy with anaesthetic and shaky with anticipation, but she is grateful that she is awake.

It has been a long morning, waiting for a non-emergency slot in the delivery theatre. Twice the orderlies fetch her and take her back. She feels light headed, has been nil-by-mouth since yesterday evening and it's after eleven-thirty when the orderlies come for the third time. In the anteroom to the theatre she is fitted with a tube for the drip, a tap jutting from the vein that runs across the top of her hand, and given an anaesthetic that will ease the pain of the epidural needle.

She is beginning to feel distant, oddly calm. She smiles up at Ben who has been given scrubs and paper shoes to wear during the caesarean.

From the delivery room comes the sound of a scream, more animal that the sound a dozen cats might make if someone stood simultaneously on their tails.

A dark man in his late fifties or early sixties puts his head in his hands and shudders. He rises stiffly from the chair where he feels he must have been sitting for half his life, and begins to pace the hospital corridor.

'Are you the father?' There is no time to reply before the bustling nurse speaks again. 'You have to wait here. No fathers allowed in.'

'I'm the mother's father. The grandfather,' Antonio says quietly to the back of the retreating nurse.

In the delivery room Consuela squats and howls, high pitched and eerie.

'Good girl, good girl.' The nurse rubs her back. 'Okay dear, you're doing fine. I'd like to listen to the baby again. I'm afraid the foetal monitor I sent for isn't working, but I can listen with this. Do you think you can just come up here a moment?'

Consuela moves compliantly towards the narrow bed that looks too high to reach, but somehow she is there, the midwife at her side, calm and encouraging. The pain in her back makes her retch as she lies back, the midwife's trumpet-like gadget feels cold and heavy against her cramping belly. She flinches, then tries to hold still.

'It's all fine, dear. Do you want to stay on the bed?'

She shakes her head, begins to move off the narrow bed, but is overtaken by the next surge of pain. It reminds her of the bellyache she had as a child once when she ate bad fish, the gut-wrenching so severe that she imagined she would die sitting on the toilet alone in the night, shivering with the shock. She wishes her mother was alive to help her through this. She wishes Jim...but the contraction overtakes thoughts of anyone else.

In the delivery theatre Megan feels a strange push, a movement that is like no sensation she can describe.

'I'm inside now and just reaching in for baby and...there we go.' The obstetrician speaks in flourishes, like a street theatre magician, Megan thinks, but at least it inspires confidence.

Megan begins to shake. She feels cold, she can feel her insides, the pressure of movement, a strange, heavy discomfort, but no pain. She can feel Ben stroking her forehead, but is too shaken to turn towards him.

'Okay Dad, here we go.' The obstetrician keeps up the steady, jolly voice.

Megan sees Ben raise the camera round his neck, hears the clicks and whirs as he stands to see over the green sheet screening her from the sight of her abdomen. She sees the tiny head of a blood-covered baby come into view above the sheet.

'...and done.'

'Three minutes four seconds,' the theatre nurse says cheerfully. She grins over at Megan. 'We keep a check on his times – fastest obstetrician in the West, we reckon.'

Megan struggles to raise her head. Across the room a midwife is rapidly weighing and washing a screaming baby.

The obstetrician smiles over the half pulled-down sheet.

'Lovely baby girl.'

'Ten,' the midwife says across the theatre.

'Perfect. The babies have a score to make sure everything is alright at birth – ten's as high as it goes.' The obstetrician grins. 'I'm going to ask my registrar to close for me, like we talked about earlier. Megan, meet

Megan.' The other Megan, a young woman with thick fair curls escaping from her tied surgeon's cap, smiles and nods.

The midwife brings the baby, wrapped, the blood wiped away, though she still has a thin wax coating in places.

'Do you think you can hold her?'

Megan nods, tears beginning to flow down her smiling, exhausted face. The midwife tucks the baby into Megan's side. Big eyes flicker open for a moment, blue, like all babies, but the darkest blue, like a clear night sky.

'Do you have a name for her?'

Megan nods. 'Elin Sarah.'

'That's lovely. Family names or just favourites?'

'Both,' Megan says.

'Lovely. She's got a sweet face hasn't she?'

'Perfect caesarean face,' the cheerful obstetrician adds, peering closer. 'They don't get crushed and bruised coming out. It's a bit of an easy ride for them in some ways, though a bit fast as well, but she's perfect.'

'Thank you. I feel... I'm sorry... I'm...'

Megan begins to shake, she can feel the room tilt, recede, she wants to ask someone to take Elin before she drops her. But the midwife is already handing her tiny, perfect daughter to Ben.

'Don't you worry, Megan. Bit of low blood pressure that's all.'

She can hear the obstetrician speaking as though he is coated in treacle, muffled, slow. She has never felt so cold.

'Our accomplished anaesthetist is right on it, little injection into your drip and you'll be right as rain.'

Megan feels nauseous; the cold is shaking her now, rattling her bones. Then a sudden sensation of being slammed at high speed into hard air, like a dip on a roller coaster. The cold melts. She feels sick, dizzy, but not shaking.

'There you go. It's a bit powerful, but you'll be fine now. Epidurals do that, lower the blood pressure and yours is already on the low side. Feeling better?'

Megan asks weakly, 'Can I hold Elin again?'

In the delivery room Consuela feels a sudden rush of something, the need to evacuate the world from between her legs. It is the most urgent feeling she has ever known.

'Yes, you can push now. Good girl.'

It is astonishing that such a push does not bring out the whole of her insides, Consuela thinks. It is unbelievable that she can push hard enough to rupture an elephant's hide and still there is no baby. The sounds seem to be coming from somewhere else, the ground shaking crescendos must be groaning out of the earth, not her body. It seems that she must be stuck here in this viscous loop of time that pushes her into a fit of urgent straining agony and pulls her back to a place of total exhaustion, and always the unearthly groaning that fills the room.

It is a shock when the baby is finally placed on her tortured stomach: slippery, covered in blood and mucous, its own piercing howl silencing the groans, the cord still pulsing inside her.

'Good girl! A lovely baby boy. Good girl. Let me just deal with this.' The midwife bends for a moment, straightens with the baby, cordless, in her arms and takes him to the other side of the room. 'I'll just get him cleaned up for you, Consuela. Well done. Just the afterbirth now, all the worst is over.'

Consuela feels dizzy, elated, exhausted, leans back on the narrow hospital bed to let the next thing happen.

'Shall I take him to his father for you while we're finishing off?'

'Father? Jim? I don't understand,' Consuela whispers weakly.

'The baby's father, Consuela. Is that him outside? He's...well...he's a little older than you.'

'My father,' Consuela says simply. 'You mean my father.'

'Ah, I see, that explains things, and your mother?'

'She died in the earthquake last July,' Consuela says almost inaudibly.

'I'm very sorry. Would your father like to hold his grandson, do you think?'

'Yes,' Consuela whispers, 'but may I? Can I see him again?'

The nurse brings the baby, already rooting at the air, his squashed face topped with a thick mane of soft, black spikes, back to Consuela.

'He is alright?'

'He's perfect.'

'Thank you.' Consuela sinks back to let the afterbirth pains take her. One last effort.

In the post-operative delivery room, Megan and Elin curl into one another on the recovery trolley. Megan can feel a whole ocean of exhaustion seeping around her, covering her slowly, lulling her. The baby, Elin Sarah, Megan reminds herself, tastes the air and blinks.

Her small hands move as though to her own internal music.

'Would you like to feed her?' The nurse holds Megan's wrist to check her pulse, puts a thermometer under her tongue, makes a note on Megan's chart. 'She looks as though she's looking for something to eat.'

'Yes.'

'Good, give me a moment and I'll come back and give you hand. Can you feel your legs yet?'

'A bit, some tingling and a kind of uncomfortable heat moving very slowly.'

'That sounds about right. I'll be with you both in a moment.'

In the post-natal suite in her bed behind paper screens, Consuela sits surrounded by white pillows, gazing at her son in his tiny Perspex crib.

'You didn't sign a release form?'

'No, I want to keep him with me.'

'Good girl. So you are going to feed him yourself?'

'Is it very hard?'

'You soon get used to it.'

'Yes.'

'Good, that's exactly what we like to hear.'

'Does he know how?'

'He will. Look, you can see him snuffling for the milk already. I have one more check to do and then I'll come and see how you are managing.'

The nurse lifts the baby into Consuela's arms.

'Hello, Edwin James.'

'Unusual names. His father is American?'

'Welsh. His father is Welsh and he will look at the stars and know that we see the same sky.'

The nurse smiles. 'I'll be one minute.'

Megan cradles the rooting baby against her breast. Her legs feel strange and heavy, the pain around her abdomen is beginning to surge into her whole body, but she feels light-headed, delirious with happiness.

'Just stroke her cheek a little, dear. She'll open her mouth and then you can slip the breast in, as far as you can, as much of the brown as you can. Never mind, dear, just stroke again; you'll soon get the hang of it.'

'That's right, Consuela, get him to open really wide. The breasts will get sore if he sucks on the end and that's when they crack and hurt. A nice big mouth is what he needs.'

Elin catches the soft mound of brown nipple deep in her tiny mouth, sucks hard. She feels the satisfying flow of warm colostrum trickle into her, gulps harder...

...so that the fine bones of his ears move in rhythmic pulses as the nourishment is sucked in. Edwin closes his eyes, a slow, ecstatic blink of luxury, and gulps again, the silk of his baby skin picking up the warmth of his mother's breast...

...so that the softness and warm liquid soothe her to sleep...

...and, sated, the breast falls from his mouth. Edwin lolls, warm and heavy in his mother's arms, oblivious and safe.

Jan Fortune-Wood is a publisher, editor and freelance creative writing tutor. Her previous novels include *Dear Ceridwen* and *The Standing Ground*. She has also written non-fiction books dealing with alternative education and parenting, the most recent being *Winning Parent, Winning Child*, and two collections of poetry, *Particles of Life* and *Stale Bread and Miracles* (a prose poetry collection). She is currently working on a poetry sequence exploring emotional connections through the landscape and architecture of an abandoned slate mining village, and a novel that ranges across three generations and two continents exploring issues of metamorphosis and identity, *I'm Still Here*. Jan lives in North Wales.